THE
CHOCOLATE
MAN

Stories

by

Randy Ross

Larod Publishing Co.
P.O. Box 30228
Los Angeles, CA 90030

Grateful acknowledgment is extended to the following publications in which some of these stories were first published: *African American Review* ("The Chocolate Man"); International Black Writers and Artists, *River Crossings* ("Red's Rhythm"); *Maryland Review* ("Grape Rain," "Conjure Women"); *Obsidian II* ("Fathers and Sons").

Library of Congress Cataloging-in-publication data

Ross, Randy
    The chocolate man: stories/ by
Randy Ross — 1st ed.
ISBN 0-9662675-0-8
1. Afro-Americans—Fiction, etc.

Printed in the United States of America

To Garry Barber —
Best regards.
[signature]
3/6/99

For Moms
(Georgiana Bassett Ross)

and

the Old Man
(Meredith Russell Ross)
1922 - 1995

To Garry Enders —
Best regards.

[signature]

3/6/99

Contents

Acknowledgments

Many individuals helped in the creation of this book. Most of the stories benefited from numerous valuable critiques provided by fellow writers participating in ongoing workshops convened by Saturday Morning Literary Workshop (SMLW) and International Black Writers and Artists (IBWA).

Gail Greer and Noma LeMoine deserve special mention. From the beginning Gail encouraged me to create more and more stories. Noma not only encouraged me to write, but also took giant steps to promote the publication of these stories.

Circa 1990, my youngest daughters, Carolyn and Lee-Madeline (both now in high school), inspired me to craft "Grape Rain," which became my first published story.

I would also like to thank *Ebony* for awarding me a $1,000 prize in the 1992 Gertrude Johnson Williams literary contest. This award enabled me to shamelessly devote more resources to my writing habit.

Several talented individuals were instrumental in the production of the book. Irwin M. Watson provided all photography. Trina Franklin designed the book's cover. Finally, Sibylla Nash copyedited the text and provided the glue that ensured the book would come to fruition.

Introduction

Randy Ross

uring my senior year at John C. Fremont High School in Los Angeles, my advanced composition teacher, Ms. Higginbottom, once asked me to write an essay on what it feels like to be black. I thought about her challenge long and hard for many days and suffered a rising vexation over my inability to trump her question with a sizzling essay. I never did write that essay. It took me years to discover why.

The Los Angeles neighborhood of my youth had been nearly all black. At the park, at church, at barbecues, at house parties, at the barbershop, at the theater, at school, and even in interactions among youth gangs—being black was being normal. Television, teachers, and cops seemed distant things visited upon the community but not of the community. Indeed, the violence, burning, and looting that saddled Los Angeles in August 1965 strengthened the camaraderie among youth within the community. So I felt even more normal than before. Had I written an essay back in 1968 about how it feels to be black, I would have been inclined to conclude, "I feel normal. I love the land, the sky, and most things in them. I love getting up in the morning to experience another day."

At the end of Summer 1973 I left Los Angeles on a Greyhound Bus headed for New York City to study public policy analysis at the State University of New York at Stony Brook. Stony Brook, Long Island differed radically from my Los Angeles community. If South Central Los Angeles were the photo, Stony Brook was its negative. In a Stony Brook supermarket in Fall 1973, a little kid looked up at me with astonishment and said, "Look, Mom, a chocolate man." This incident and other "colorful" interactions provide fodder for the short story, "The Chocolate Man," which was first published in *African American Review* (1994, 28:3)

The "Chocolate Man," and the other fictions contained in this book represent a collective response to Ms. Higginbottom's challenge. These stories are fictions largely because of my psychological need to plow regularity out of chaos or to inject passion into mundaneness. Truth often finds its way into fiction. But as a writer of fiction, I am predisposed to bending truth. Truth well bent superimposes itself onto reality in a way that transforms fragments of life, time, and space into something more daring, glorifying, and enlightening.

Enjoy.

The

Chocolate

Man

Randy Ross

man, standing high above a toilet peeing, stares in the wall-to-wall bathroom mirror of his new upscale apartment. *The image in the mirror is over six feet tall, not quite thirty, athletic and energetic, well-educated, wellpaid, single, and proud. The man smiles at the image faintly and says, "You're okay." The image points at the man and replies, "No, brother, you're okay."*

* * * * *

It's noon Sunday and I have slummed away whole sheets of morning on my twentieth floor terrace trying to make sense of what happened to me yesterday...or, depending on how you look at it, what did not happen. My maiden jaunt through my new community, Bay View, was either a carpeted introduction or a stinging slap in the face. I can't decide which; and it matters dearly. It's the difference between inclusion and exclusion, night and day, stop and go, sanity and schizophrenia.

My loose-fitting navy blue sweat shorts and pineapple tank top flap in the breeze. Dark shades and a tinted acrylic terrace wall shield my eyes from the sun. Arms crossed, legs crossed, I sway in a giving chaise longue in meter with the elegant ripples of glossy blue waves that comb the bay, oblivious to the din of the pedestrians way down below. Occasionally I pat my sandaled feet on the carpeted terrace floor to the straight-ahead, post-bop jazz streaming through stereophonic speakers in the living room.

I peer at the bay and the thought comes and goes that Bay View needs a lot more trees, shrubbery, and wildly growing things. Unfortunately, the idea is twisted with hypocrisy. My old Queens neighborhood had hardly any public plant life to speak of—a tree here, another there, reeds of grass squeezing through cracks in the sidewalk slabs that dominated the streets. On the other hand, Bay View is generously peppered with all sorts of flora—conifers, bloated shrubbery, ivy galore. The first time I gaped at Bay View from my terrace, I exclaimed to my girlfriend, Fifi, "Why so many trees?" But now that I have been secularly baptized in my new surroundings, I no longer feel this community has enough plant life. I would prefer that Bay View be thatched densely enough to quench my newfound thirst for privacy. Toward that end, I have contemplated foresting my terrace.

However, I must be considerate of my shapely, tangerine-breasted next-door neighbor, Susan Bayer. The verdant blotting of the translucent acrylic partition separating our contiguous terraces might be taken as a vile reenactment of Jim Crow cowardly hiding behind nature's dress. My built-in historical baggage would not allow me to brook the devilish fellow, so how could I expect my neighbor to accept him? But, who knows, perhaps she would applaud whatever initiative I took to buttress our division.

I suspect Dr. Bayer will come out, as usual,

at six on the dot, to bask, too, but separately, in an ebbing sun—her own shrubs, her chaise, her flowers in their bulging pots, her sunshades resting securely on the huge braid of hair running laterally across the top of her head. I would not be surprised if she did not say "Hello" today. Though not unpopular in this swirling city, the naked proximity of our contrasting skin complexions fosters uneasiness. But on the ground, the earth level, it is safe to say "Hi," smile broadly, and chat but briefly.

But height creates social distance, no matter how near the chocolate and cream-colored fingers. The higher the floor, the greater the uneasiness. Black and white. Beige and more beige. The wall dividing our terraces symbolizes the madness. I have lived here now for two weeks. The first time we met, we looked, smiled, exchanged identification, backed away from the wall, and thereafter each of us has assumed the other does not exist.

Perhaps her glass door will slide open a bit before or after six. If it does, I will ask if she's had dinner. If she is receptive, I will invite her over for baked chicken. If, as usual, she comes out at six sharp, I will assume the pattern sticks and cordially disregard her.

*   *   *   *   *

The weekend had begun with a bang. Friday afternoon, backed by a team of super management analysts, I gift-wrapped the findings of an exhaustive yearlong management study and proffered recommendations that, if implemented, promised resuscitation of the client's shaky bottom line. After a debriefing session back at our Midtown Manhattan office, my associates and I celebrated at a nearby watering hole with salty pretzels and the happy-hour libations needed to wash them down. A couple of beers into the celebration, I rose from the bar stool and bid everyone goodnight and a rejuvenating weekend. Draping my wool-lined London Fog over one arm and carrying my briefcase in the other, I exited the bar and stepped toward the subway station. For the first time in weeks, work would not follow me home. My briefcase was empty; my head was light. Roseate over the success of the day and cherishing the potential promise of things to come, I shunned the train and hailed a taxi with the haughty confidence of a person who lived in a New York community where cabbies are well tipped and never mugged.

"Where to?"

"Bay View, please."

*   *   *   *   *

Early Saturday, I had hopped out of bed filled with playful energy. Rapt by the bay's beauty and mild temperament, I showered, put on my most colorful jogging suit and sneakers, opened the refrigerator and gulped down several ounces of orange juice from the half-gallon carton, then walked bouncily to the elevator whistling. Downstairs, I asked the pompously uniformed doorman for the shortest route to the jogging path that rimmed the bay. His directions and animated gestures seemed unnecessarily flowery for a day meant for relaxation. As I walked leisurely in the appointed direction, an entrance to the path revealed itself. It was there that I lifted my legs and began my first excursion along the bay.

After gobbling up a few miles of breathtaking scenery, I turned and jogged across a bridge that led back to the mainland. Catching my breath and wiping at the sweat on my face, I stopped at a nearby supermarket to grab a six-pack of Diet Coke. When I stepped on the entrance mat and the automatic door buzzed open, a cooled warm breeze ran liquid peppermint through my pores. Preparing myself for the soda search, I could not help but notice a little guy tiptoeing, extending his arm and body, reaching intently into his mom's shopping cart for something he yearned or was curious about. He was a cherub little fellow, auburn curly hair, wearing a spiffy green jump suit.

"Harold! Get down from there!" his mother commanded.

The little guy just kept tiptoeing and reaching.

"How are ya little fella?" I said.

Harold craned his neck, the metal spokes of the shopping cart blurring as his eyes caught on to me.

He looked at once puzzled and amazed.

I smiled and peered up the aisle before me in search of the soda.

Then Harold cried out, "Look, Mom, a chocolate man!"

Heads turned. Harold's mom, in her excitement, accidentally dismantled an elaborate saltine cracker display, turning toward her son as if the world were crumbling merely to say "Shhhhhh." I felt embarrassed because Harold's mom seemed embarrassed. She never did face my way. Instead, she busied herself juggling cracker boxes.

Chocolate man? That was the first time I had been called that...must be the African, Native American, and European mingling in my skin, reddened by the sun, and glossed over by sweat dripping from my brow. My jogging along the bay at a moderately brisk pace had not given my new neighbors much of a gander at me. But now that I had paused in the market, I could be ogled more easily.

Little Harold kept right on looking at me puzzled and amazed, still standing on his toes, his hands still clasping the rim of the shopping cart.

The other shoppers suavely ignored the complication by looking away without really looking away. Even then, they probably looked only because they wondered what in the world was a chocolate man. I wondered, too, and wished I had a mirror to see myself.

Quite frankly, I appreciated the way little Harold had looked at me. There was a twinkle in his eyes. As I moved through the store, I even wondered if I should be amused. If I was the least bit disturbed, it was with everyone except Harold. Presumably their nonchalance represented a sort of tacit apology. But an apology

seemed out of order. A broad smile would have
been fitting.

After all, little Harold had not called me a
spook. He had called me a "chocolate man."
Was not his reference Hershey's or Nestle's milk
chocolate? The more I thought about it, the better I felt. Yet I could not convey my mild elation
to any of those who thought it fitting to se-
quester themselves from what they consensually
perceived to be a racial indelicacy. They would
not have understood, because, at least at that
moment, they were not positioned to understand. So I just winked at little Harold. I
wanted him to know that everything was just
fine.

* * * * *

Back at the luxury high-rise, my new home,
a six pack of soda tucked under my arm, I
awaited an elevator with a neighbor.

"These elevators are dreadfully slow," he
complained.

"Yep."

"Live here long?" he asked.

"No, just a couple of weeks."

"How do you like it so far?"

"Fine."

"Although you must admit the rent is somewhat on the high side," he probed.

"Au contraire," I lied. "I personally can't believe the rent is so low."

"Oh." He paused momentarily. "Are you
the footballer?"

"The footballer?"

"Yeah, there's a guy here who plays professional football for the New York Jets."

"Is that right? Well, I enjoy sports, but I am not a professional football player. I guess there is more than one of us here."

"One of what?"

"You know."

"Oh."

* * * * *

Later Saturday afternoon, I invited Fifi over for lunch. As usual she had a lot to say.

"Baby, this twentieth floor terrace is heaven ...a romantic vista. A bird's nest! Look at the tanned bodies sprawled along the luxurious swimming pool; the hexagonal refreshment stand...mai tai, ummmm.... The water and the boats that dot the bay—big ones, small ones—look at them. Oh, baby, it is wonderful here."

Fifi keeps telling me how crazy she is about this place. While that pleases me, it doesn't affect my countenance, because my moving to the Bay View Luxury Apartments was her idea, not mine.

"Now aren't you glad you left all that squalor behind?"

"Squalor?"

Now why did I go and say that? I had succeeded, as I often do, in screwing up the mood. Fifi clasped her disarming denim-hugged hips, and her mouth shifted into overdrive.

"Don't play dumb. That creepy Queens neighborhood you lived in was the pits."

"It's not the pits, Fifi. Real people live

there. So how can it be the pits?"

"It's the pits because it stunk."

"It stunk?"

"The garbage, the crime, the noise, the traffic; you name it, it stunk."

For the two weeks I've been here and sometime before, I have argued with Fifi about this matter. Really, I am not very determined to win these arguments and she knows it. As soon as she starts throwing her miniature temper tantrums, I give in.

You see, the move from "squalor" to "luxury" has stirred my conscience. You don't make things better by leaving. As an octogenarian city councilman used to say back in Los Angeles, "Don't move! Improve!" But according to Fifi, the old neighborhood was a real downer, absolutely no hope. I didn't budge, so she threatened me.

"Move or else...!"

The threat came while I was in a particularly vulnerable position; so I pecked Fifi on the neck and swore I would look for a better place immediately. Of course, she had already searched for and found the new land, Bay View. Before I knew what hit me, I was here.

When I pined over the high rent, Fifi discarded my concern with a hand wave that just as well could have been used to swat a fly. "That's not your problem, ba-by...maybe someone else's. So don't worry about it. You're a management consultant with unlimited potential. Besides you didn't kill yourself getting all those college degrees for nothing. Enjoy it; enjoy me."

"What about my friends," I argued, "do I callously forsake them?"

The question had the impact of a vacuous thud. My friends are my friends no matter where I live. Aren't they? Truthfully, I loved my old Los Angeles and Queens neighborhoods. They were more like home than this place by the bay. In them, I had not felt like a minority. Fifi peeped the emptiness in my argument and lit into me.

"Forsake them? If they had the chance, they'd do the same thing you did and invite you over for cocktails. I don't see why you don't just let go of that inner-city cultural bullshit. You know good and well you adore this place, you fraud. That's what's wrong with you high-yellow Negroes; you never know whether you're going or coming."

"Fifi!"

I had prepared an absolutely scrumptious baked chicken—marinated twenty-four hours in all sorts of wonderful herbs and spices, golden brown crispy skin. But she talked so much, the chicken got cold. My appetite froze, so I didn't slice it. We didn't eat and she left. What the hell.

*　*　*　*　*

Fifi having gone in a huff, I felt edgy and courageous enough to give tennis another whack. On the first court, the tennis pro enthusiastically measured out a lesson to a middle-aged woman who behaved as if she had read books on tennis etiquette. Of the remaining four courts, only one was occupied—a short, stocky, blond-haired gentleman was practicing his service. In my eagerness to play, I asked him if he'd like to "hit a few."

"Of course," he replied.

Thirty minutes into our game, a zinging tennis ball deflected off my racket onto the core of my eye socket. I wanted to call it a night. But my ad hoc partner, Huntz, insisted I give my eye a rest; in maybe ten minutes, the blurred vision and the headache would go away and we could resume play.

While sitting about an umbrella-enfolded patio table, I nursed my eye while Huntz spouted verbal palliatives. During our chit-chat, Huntz recounted his recent six-day vacation to Puerto Rico. On his first day, he had dozed off on the beach for four hours and awakened with what he thought were third-degree sunburns.

"Gee, I would have died under those circumstances," I said.

"No, probably not," Huntz said. "I understand that your people have an extra layer of skin that protects you from the sun's rays."

Without a clear thought, all I could think to say was "Oh." Then I asked him how he happened upon that knowledge.

"It is true," he said. "That is why you are not as affected by the heat as I am."

I suggested to Huntz that the reason the sun tolerated my skin more than his had nothing to do with the thickness of my skin.

"But you do have an extra layer of skin," Huntz insisted.

Quite frankly, I had no idea whether Huntz was right or wrong. I had never in life heard anything like it. But having become a chocolate man, a professional football player, and a high-yellow Negro in the space of a day, I was a tad suspicious and scrappy. Picking at his logic, I suggested that since albinos are doubly sensitive to the sun's rays, their skin must be thinnest.

"Hmm, I had not thought of that," Huntz said, nudging his upper lip with an index finger.

Adding another layer to this "layer" question, I noted that some albinos are black and, therefore, some blacks have thinner skins than whites.

"Hmmmm," he muttered.

And I "hmm-ed," too.

"Then what is the reason . . .?"

Before Huntz could complete his question, I had blurted out the word "pigmentation." I pointed out that he and I had different levels of melanin in our skins. The more melanin, the greater one's resistance to the sun's rays.

"But I'm white, I have no pigmentation, no melanin."

"Albinos are white; you do have color."

"Really?" he laughed.

"Frankly, we're very nearly the same complexion."

He laughed again. I laughed, too.

"So what might my complexion be?" he said.

"Brown, tan, beige. Take your pick."

"Well, now, what's yours?" he asked.

I was stomped. It didn't seem appropriate to say brown, tan, or beige. So I told him that my color was chocolate.

"Chocolate?"

"Sure, why not?"

"Okay," he laughed. "That's a nice color. Your eye looks better now. Come. Let us hit more balls before the night says 'No.'"

* * * * *

After a remarkably colorful Saturday, I have somehow zombied my way into Sunday. As Bay View spins away from the sun, my sense of self still eludes me. However, I take solace in having the means to deal with my dilemma up high in private. For the higher one lives, the fewer people there are.

Indeed, the true value of lofty abodes lies not in their provision of panoramic vistas of this stupendous city, or in getting one nearer to heaven. Rather, they enable those of us who can afford them to get away from it all—the maddening crowd, the heavy air of excessive personalities—perhaps a necessity if you perceive acutely that you are just one among an uncountable number of unknowable people, all literally within eyeshot. Here, if one cared to, the trappings of culture and etiquette could be dropped. Basic courtesies and facades could be eructed from the soul. Up high, there is simply no need to hold heavy gas in the bowels, massage a martini, and simultaneously chat with a pseudo interest in the politics of the District of Columbia.

You see, gas rises toward the stratosphere, toward heaven; cultural facades fall downward at the same speed as bricks (according to Newton).

So I'm up here airing out, feeling lofty but unsettled on who I am, and occasionally reflecting on the tension that grips the translucent dividing wall. Yet the wall could not have been meant for me, or against me, but rather for separateness' sake. Up high, it is not common to see a chocolate man basking in the sun...alone. Under these conditions, a beige young woman could not be protected by the earthly ethos of artificial cordiality. I was for some days a stranger, then she got the make on me (purely for security reasons). Now, to her, I'm a model neighbor (quiet and nonexistent).

I think perhaps I'll break the pattern tonight...even if she comes out at six sharp. After all, how could she not like chocolate — unless she's on a diet? But maybe she knows Huntz. I hope she doesn't know Fifi. I would prefer that she knew little Harold, for chocolate is a lot brighter than high-yellow.

Red's

Rhythm

Randy Ross

oy, what you know about dancing? Just 'cause you got a little college beyond your belt don't mean you the best stepper on the floor. Why, if she were still livin', your grandma could have told you about me — but I don't know if she would have. In my time, they called me Red. I was mercurial...hot as blue fire. I could reel on swamp mud at two hundred miles an hour and stop straight up on a Canadian dime. I used to spin my body so fast that I woulda drilled a hole clean through that floor you're high-steppin' on, and the sparks flyin' from my taps woulda scared away all the critters from under the house.

You don't believe me, do you? Well listen up!

Back in New Orleans, in-folk supped jazz music for lunch and imbibed it for dinner to wash down gumbo so spicy hot it would make you sweat. So usually when the last set ended at the High Seven Club, the hip cats — after gumbo, jazz, and wine — strutted through the door mopping their faces with oversized handkerchiefs. The ladies of course had powdered up and cooled off long before the music stopped.

One Saturday night, me and Raynell "Dizzy" Williams exited the High Seven and made our way toward an after-hours jam I had been invited to by a sweet cube of sugar named Sarah G. who, earlier in the evening, had tried her best to keep up with me on the dance floor. We finally made it to the joint—a ritzy multistory tenement that looked like a private museum. As soon as I knocked on the door, the brass peephole squeaked open. I felt eyes and air poring through on me.

"Red here. Sarah G. plugged me."

The door opened and big Charlie Downs, dockworker by day and bouncer by night, towered over me with a grin.

"My man, Red, the jazzy high-stepper."

"The one and only." I removed my cocked Panama from my slicked-down hair. "And this here is my running ace, Dizzy."

"Y'all come on through."

"Solid."

I flipped Charlie two bits, and me and Dizzy eased down the hallway toward the sound of the groove. Before we could figure which way to go, a smiling petite waitress wearing a tight skirt above her knees had come up and handed me a glass of watered-down whisky on the rocks.

"Hi, mister high-stepper."

"Hi to you, doll. Red's my name."

"Everybody knows that."

As Dizzy lifted a drink for himself from the tray and replaced it with a coin, I looked around at the hip people in the room we had landed in, gestured a toast, downed my shot of whiskey in a single swallow, then looked over at the waitress for a refill.

Only the squares didn't get juiced. Red was no square, so I got down, real down—high as Ben Franklin's kite. A few more shots of whiskey layered on early evening wine had me feelin' good as a pig in slop. There I was tripping off the funny lights in a large multidimensional room peppered with in-folk. The players huddled in corners floating in their baggy pleated pants and flashing their gold watch chains. A few cats leaned so far forward that if their ladies hadn't propped'em up, they'da fallen flat on their mugs.

Dizzy got caught up in a lively corner discussion with a few musician acquaintances who couldn't resist trying to unravel Charlie Parker's solos. So I got my swollen, woozy head out of that scene and hitched a ride here and there on some of those ad hoc confab cliques continually forming and dismantling in other corners, in other rooms, on upper floors, and on the roof.

A cool breeze swirled around on the roof. But hot music and jammed-tight congestion warmed all bodies — big bodies, little bodies, wide and short bodies, tall bodies, curvaceous bodies, blob bodies, liquid and some dry bodies, lean and foaming bodies, scented bodies, working bodies, somebodies, and nobodies. I bet you didn't know there was that many different kind of bodies. They had more than that congregating on the roof that summer morning, but I just can't remember them right off.

Then there was one lovely body I'll never forget. I can see her this very moment the way I saw her that night way back yonder...stuffed like Louisiana hot sausage, seasoned with sage and other mouth-watering spices. I can see her just as clearly as I can see you slip and slide and jerk across them varnished wooden slats on your mama's living room floor. Early that Sunday morning, the lady circled deliciously about a barrel of fire center roof to the beat of a seductive number blaring out of the arch-headed jukebox. Hundreds of skinny braids flung about her aerodynamic noggin like an iridescent tetherball seen through hallucinating eyes. Liquid magic flew from each twirling braid. The crowd barked with pleasure, clapped and egged her on.

I said to myself, what is this wholesome, beautiful goddess doing shaking her lithe physique that way? I couldn't believe such a tall, wide, curvaceous body could be so foaming, working, and liquid. She had to be into yoga, aerobics, voodoo, or something. This thing she was working on churned my machismo. What she was doing was Red's kind of thing. Congo Square ain't gone nowhere.

Gingerly I pranced out to center roof and emphatically introduced myself.

"Red here, baby! What you say?"

She looked me straight in the eye and smiled. "You is red, ain't you, but are you hot?"

What was she looking at? A sunburned grape? She could not have been looking at me. I am not red; this shirt is red.

I peeled off my suede jacket, draped it across my shoulder, and primed up for the lady's sultry challenge.

"Didn't I say my name was Red?"

"Yeah. But are you red-dy?"

"Anytime. Any way. I was born steppin', and ain't nothing slowed me down yet."

I slung my jacket across the room, undid the top buttons on my red silk shirt, and bared my heaving chest. Then I snapped my fingers in beat with the polyrhythmic sounds that lit up the roof and the blackened sky.

She faced my way and snapped her fingers, too.

"Well, honey, get down and hit it. 'Cause if you can't hit it, you can't get it."

I wanted to ask "Get what?" It would have been a natural question, but square as a checkerboard. Red was too cool for that. Snapped my fingers to the beat and dipped my knees. That's what I did.

Suddenly I whirled my body around slowly. I had one hand all the way down fingers snapping, and I had the other hand all the way up fingers snapping. I moved about her smoldering, gyrating mass to map out the territory, all the while smiling and peering into her large, airy dark eyes, mindful that the popping crowd was gearing up for show time. Those who knew my reputation chanted my name. "Red," they said. But to my surprise, some high cascading voices in the crowd echoed brickhouse's name cacophonously.

"Ruby, Ruby."

"Ru-bay, honey get down."

Then I heard Sarah G.'s voice.

"Ruby, show that stud a thing or two, but not too much, 'cause he learns real fast."

Ruby! The name caught my ear. They say she had been all over twisting that wonderfully supple body. In Harlem at the Savoy. In Los Angeles at Club Alabam. Now I was looking at her with my very own eyes. Uptown and down.

Live and in person. Done tasted the salt of the
Atlantic and the Pacific. Ruby. Come to con-
quer Orleans.

But Orleans was my town! Me, Red, who
hung out with the high-steppin' Copas and blew
all the young girls' minds with my flying feet
and mercurial hips.

So I told her again, "Red's my name, baby.
Yeah. From coast to coast. Every day." All the
while, I still snapped my fingers low and high
while circling my prey.

She moved toward me as if she were gliding
through air. Then she caught me off guard with
her magical smile, banged my poor little mes-
merized body hard with her thick hips, and
whispered within a hot breath of my lips.

"Olé."

*   *   *   *   *

Just look at your grandpa. Don't look like
it, but I used to be the baddest ace of spades ever
'lit on that Creole plantation. Me, Red. Could
spin so fast on my tips that if I didn't stop, next
thing you'd hear a siren come to put out the fire.
I was good. When I got good and hot, they called
me Red. At my peak, I scorched...turned ice
blue. Then they called me Cool Red. And God
gave Noah the rainbow sign, no more water, Red
next time.

You don't believe me, do you?

Well anyway, son, the truth is that dancing
and rhythm are glued together with life...like
red beans and rice. And during the hardest of
times — which I've had my share of in this life

of mine — rhythm can dress up the worst kind of noise.

Long before you ever think about getting as old as me, you're going to find out that you can no longer hang your cool on the golden hanger. That's when you'll move over to silver or copper. You may even lose a step or two. Take the day your mother came into this world. I can see her now...her soft little body curled up in your grandma's arms. That was the day I gave up trippin' and juicin' altogether and settled down like regular folks.

But the rhythm that started in me is still in me. It's all up in my head and ain't go'n never go away. It defines and creates the harmony in my soul. It's a gift, an inheritance that moves along from generation to generation. I can hear it in your music and see it in your dance. And no matter how many college degrees you end up getting, that rhythm will always be with you.

Just to think, it all started in the wee hours of a warm Sunday morning when a pretty lump of sugar banged my hips and had me stumbling around a barrel of fire. I'll tell you the truth. Your grandma Ruby wore me out on that roof, but she fixed my soul for keeps. Sweetness, goodness, may she forever rest in peace.

Randy Ross

Grape

Rain

Randy Ross

rs. Taylor gripped her hips and stared down at her grandson with squinting, angry eyes.

"Now, Michael, let me and the world get your story straight," she teethed with restraint. "The reason you all wet up with a sick stomach is 'cause you was jumping up and catching grapes in the rain by the railroad tracks with an old man named Frank?"

"But Ma'Dear, that's what really happened," Mike pleaded.

"To the bush, Michael Taylor! Now!"

"Aw, Ma'Dear," Mike whined. "It's raining outside and my stomach feels real sick."

"Never mind the rain; you already wet. Never mind your stomach; your behind's go'n feel worse than that when I get that switch on it."

His grandmother didn't believe his story. The way she described it, Mike wasn't sure he believed it either.

"I want you to get me the biggest switch you can find on that bush."

Dejectedly, Mike dragged his feet outside in the rain to the big bush on the side of the house and yanked off a branch large enough to keep him from having to go back outside to get another one.

"Michael, I am real angry with you," began Mrs. Taylor as she stripped the wet leaves from the thick branch. "First, you go outside in a pouring down rain when you should know better. Then you stay out so long you got me worried sick. But worse, you come home and lie to me. If you lie to me, you'll lie to God."

Mike's arms stung from the hard lashes. His grandmother was right; after the whipping, his stomach didn't seem to hurt so much. Other parts of his body hurt worse.

"Now go to your room and take off those wet clothes."

As Mrs. Taylor watched her grandson lumber to his bedroom with a sniffling, bowed head, worry crept into her face.

"God, please spare Michael the plight of his father," she prayed. "Let him know the world, know its reality, and know his place in it."

* * * * *

After removing his clothes, Mike flopped wearily on his bed and thought about what had happened to him.

That morning, the wind had whistled under a gloomy sky, and an occasional flashing light had augured a heavy, hard downpour. Things were different after a hard rain. A good rain redecorates the world. But because it usually clears up so quickly, you never get a chance to experience all the new furniture.

Mike wanted to see how quickly the rain would deflower the dandelions and how close to the ground it would press the wild grass near the railroad tracks.

He thirsted for a taste of a big rain. Would it have the crystal purity of well water? Would the smog give it a smoky flavor, or would this rain be larger than smog?

Mike wanted to smell the rain, hear up close the sounds it creates when hitting rocks, cardboard, glass bottles, pipes, stucco, telephone poles, grass, grounded objects. So after he finished his chores and watched his favorite Saturday morning television shows, he put on his jacket and headed outside for the railroad tracks.

*   *   *   *   *

The darkened sky filled with chicken-footed lightening and booming thunder, and the rain started coming down by the bucket. Mike ran for cover under a jutting tin roof that sounded like a thousand pigeons were dancing on it.

"Hear the drums?" a voice asked.

"What?" Mike uttered in surprise, turning around quickly to see an old man under the tin roof sitting casually on a milk crate, looking nowhere but everywhere, sipping from a small silver flask.

"The drums," repeated the old man. "You hear 'em?"

"Who are you?" Mike said, standing at the edge of the tin roof.

"Just an old traveler."

"I never saw you before. You live here?"

"I grew up 'round here long time ago. Been travelin' for a spell, but I pass through now and then."

"You know anybody from here?"

"Lots of people, I reckon. If they still around."

"So who you come to see?"

"Nobody in particular. Just passing through is all."

"How you get here?"

"Come by train."

"You take the train a lot?"

"Sure. All the time."

"What places you been on the train?"

"Everywhere. I done seen more of these United States than most people will get a chance to see in a lifetime. But then sometimes I feel I ain't been nowhere. It depends on how you look at it."

"Have you seen the White House?"

"Naw, but I've been pretty close. Down south, I've seen bigger places than the White House. They call 'em plantations."

"Plantations?"

"Yeah. Big farms where the old Africans labored. Our kinfolks. Where they picked the cotton and the cotton pricked their fingers and scratched their souls. I seen all this and a lot more. Like I say, I been everywhere but I ain't been nowhere. That's because everywhere I been our forefathers already been there."

Mike didn't understand all the old man was saying. But something about the way he was saying it made Mike want to keep listening.

"Yeah, son, you can go lots of places by train. I done seen all kinds of trains and all kinds of tracks. And I done worked on trains and I done worked on tracks. I done worked where they make the rails and the tie plates. I 'member when they made rails that was shorter than you but weighed twice as much. Now they got rails longer than a oak tree, so heavy a mule couldn't carry 'em. There used to be tracks around here so narrow even a boy your size could run on top of 'em two at a time. Now the gauge between most tracks done stretched out to 'bout the length of your body. I've seen rails where the crossties was so far apart, Jesse Owens couldn't jump from one to the next. Now the ties so close together, it's hard to run fast down the middle of the track without jumping over 'em."

A gust of wind swept rain over the tin roof, and Mike remembered that his grandmother had warned him not to get wet. The big lumps of rain that pounded the ground resembled the craggy rocks that surrounded the railroad tracks, but they hardly made a sound when they fell. When he looked at the ground from the shelter of the tin roof, he saw nothing but water.

Forgetting his grandmother's warning, Mike trotted into the rain to take a closer look. He couldn't believe what he thought he saw — grapes raining down from the sky.

But that can't be, he thought, as he cleared water from his face and eyes.

Yet, he saw them. He reached for the falling gray-green grapes with his outstretched hands, but all he got was a pounding from the rain.

Mike went closer to the tracks where he thought he saw bunches of grapes pouring down. He opened his mouth and tried to catch some. But when the falling lumps touched his mouth, Mike darted away. Everything was coming down so fast and hard. He tried catching grapes in his hands again, but got nothing. Then he opened his mouth again. This time, he closed his eyes shut and tensed his facial muscles to allay the sting of the juice that would surely splatter. The sharp beads of fast flying liquid hit his face furiously as he smacked his lips with the rhythm of the rain.

Still smacking his lips for the taste of grapes, Mike ran back under the shelter of the tin roof. He inspected his hands, front and back, but saw nothing. He put his hands to his nose.

"Everything all right, son?"

"Grapes are out there," Mike blurted faintly. Then he looked out toward the railroad tracks where he thought the grapes were raining down. The rain was so thick it blocked off a clear view of the tracks from the shed. But he thought he could make out the grapes still coming down.

The old man stared out at the rain and the tracks, too. But he didn't say anything. He just nodded his head several times, unscrewed the top on his flask and took another sip, screwed the cap back on, and then wiped his mouth with his hands.

"Ain't wine made out of grapes?" Mike asked.

"Most times."

"Can I try it?"

"Best to leave it alone, son."

"Why do you drink wine?"

"Well, first of all, what um drinking is corn liquor, but it's just as bad as wine. Then, second of all, there's no answer I could give you that could help you any. 'Cept to say that I been drinking this stuff for a long time. In the beginning, it filled my head with 'tata puddin' dreams. Now this old hooch just keeps my body from shaking, but most times it haunts me with bitter memories."

"Why are you out here all by yourself in the rain?" Mike said.

"It's peaceful out here. Nobody around to mess with me, to mess with my space. Besides, there's too much history in them tracks for me to get bored. If you plant your ear just right on top of the rail, you can hear John Henry driving spikes, corn-fed livestock moaning off to slaughter, train whistles, and steel wheels clanging down the tracks."

"Who is John Henry?"

"John Henry? He just a hard working man."

Mike strained to get a clear view of the tracks. Grapes were falling by the bunch, it seemed. He had yet to taste them; perhaps the rain did not want him to. Perhaps there really weren't any grapes out there. Maybe it was all in his mind. Then he remembered something his grandpa had told him: "Odds are meant to be beat or bucked, and if they aren't beat or bucked, then they're still odds." So Mike ran back out into the grape rain.

The old man marveled at Mike's persistence for a while before he got up and walked outside into the rain, kneeled down, and planted his ear flat on a rail.

"Son, there's a bunch happening in these

tracks today. Nothing like a good, strong rain to wake 'em up."

Following the man's lead, Mike placed an ear over a railroad track. He listened hard but didn't get as excited as the old man about the reverberating, cavernous sounds that flowed through the tracks. So Mike got right back up and kept fishing for grapes.

Later, the old man snailed back to the tinned-roof shelter, sat on the milk crate, sipped from his flask, and watched Mike pursue his quest. After a while, the old man went back out into the rain and bent down by the tracks to pick up a small rock.

"Son, you okay?"

"Yes, sir."

"By the way, what's your name?" the man said, as he pitched a rock along the tracks.

"Michael."

"Well, Michael, you better go on home now before you catch the pneumonia or something worse. You had a good go at it. Other opportunities will come your way. Just keep right on trying and you'll find your way."

Michael stood alternately daydreaming and listening to the old man. Something was out there and there was more to find out about it. But another layer of darkness blanketed the sky. By now his grandmother was probably prancing wondering where he was.

"What's your name?" Michael said.

"Frank's my name. Glad to make the acquaintance."

"Did you see the grapes?"

"Nope. But that don't mean you ain't seen 'em. A lot of stuff in life is that way. If you saw grapes falling, felt them on your tongue, and heard them when they splattered, then grapes was falling. So go on home and don't worry about it."

Sneakers squishing with rain water and jeans muddied, Mike pulled up the collar of his jacket over his ears and began the walk home.

"See you around," Mike said.

The old man walked slowly back toward the tinned-roof shed. "Okay," he said.

* * * * *

Mike had been asleep for about an hour by the time his grandfather came home. Mr. Taylor went to the bathroom, relieved himself, washed his hands, then went to the kitchen and sat down at the dinette. Mrs. Taylor served him a plate of fried chicken, biscuits, and blackeye peas.

"Michael came home all wet. Say he had a stomach ache from eating too many grapes."

"Oh, yeah? Where is he now?"

"In his room sleep."

"He all right?"

"I reckon so."

"He'll be all right. He's tough like Donald was."

"Well, he's like Donald in a lot of ways."

"Yep."

"He came in here talkin' about seein' stuff that just can't be. Like Donald used to."

"No foolin'," replied Mr. Taylor taking a bite

out of a piece of fried chicken.

"Say he saw grapes comin' down out of the sky."

"Must be seein' things I reckon," said Mr. Taylor scooping some blackeye peas into his spoon. "How grapes go'n be falling out of the sky? Next thing you know, he'll say they had parachutes on 'em."

Mrs. Taylor, eyed her husband suspiciously. "Why you say that?"

"Say what?"

"Parachutes."

"I don't know, Nettie. It just popped into my mind."

"Well, anyway I whipped his butt somethin' good and sent him to his room." Mrs. Taylor placed a glass of lemonade on the table for her husband. "Come in here with that mess. I tell you that boy worries me. That's the way his father started. Seeing things that ain't. People started rumoring he was crazy even before he jumped."

"Like I say, Nettie, Donald was not crazy. The problem is that some things people say 'ain't,' really 'is.' A lot of Donald's 'ises' was their 'ain'ts.' He strove to see beyond the mundane. You understand what I'm saying Nettie?"

"Jumping off Jasper bridge was everybody's 'ain't'," Mrs. Taylor said.

"Depends on how you look at it. In my way of thinking, Donald flew off Jasper bridge with the wingspan of an eagle."

"Damn it, Joe, he jumped."

"No, Nettie, my boy flew off Jasper. And it

had to be some kind of beautiful. But as he soared, somebody told him that Negroes couldn't fly, and he believed it. That's when he got scared, fell, and killed his self."

"Mister, you ain't got a bit of sense. You go'n go to your grave believin' that mess."

"Well, Nettie," said Mr. Taylor putting down his biscuit, "you remember Donald your way and I'll 'member him mine. But one thing for sure, he was our boy. Let's leave it right there."

Mrs. Taylor pivoted to the sink to wash the dishes and began humming Amazing Grace. Mr. Taylor sniffled and pulled a checkered handkerchief from his back pants pocket to blow his nose.

"The boy say he met an old man down by the tracks named Frank."

Mr. Taylor stirred in his seat. "Frank Jones?"

"Ain't nobody seen Frank Jones in years," Mrs. Taylor said. "He probably dead and in his grave by now. Must be somebody else."

"I reckon I was the last to see him 'round this way. That was eleven, twelve years ago, 'bout the time Michael come into this world. He looked plenty alive to me.

"Did Mike eat before he went to sleep?"

"No, he went straight to bed after I whipped his hindpa'ts."

"Fix him a plate," Mr. Taylor calmly insisted. "Um go'n take it to him."

*　*　*　*　*

"Michael!"

"Hunh?"

"Get up and have something to eat."

"I don't feel good, Grandpa."

"Well, when you get some food in your stomach, you'll feel a lot better. Come on, get up. I got a plate for you. Here, hold these plates and um'o get us some lemonade."

Mike sat up on the side of his bed and reached for the two plates and his grandfather went back to the kitchen.

On returning, Mr. Taylor set two tall glasses of lemonade on the nightstand, sat down in a chair by the bed, got his plate from Mike, and continued to eat.

"Son, your grandma's fried chicken and biscuits can't be beat."

Mike kept his eyes down on his plate, nibbled at the chicken and biscuits, and listened, knowing that his grandmother had told his grandpa what had happened. His grandpa came into the room to talk sometimes, but never with food. Grandma didn't tolerate that. So she must have told him.

"Your grandma told me what happened." Mr. Taylor sliced the air with his right hand. "You know she don't believe in too much if it ain't right straight down the middle. If it's way over this way, she don't want to have nothing to do with it. If it's way over that way, she don't want to have nothing to do with it. Her philosophy is, if you keep with the straight and narrow, then you keep yourself, you keep your mind.

"Well, now, my point of view is different. I believe that if everybody just walked the middle

line, this old world of ours would be real
crowded but empty, automatic, and just plain
boring. In a manner of thinking, a tree is just a
trunk unless people branch out to give it an
identity. Your grandma, like most people in the
world, is folded in with the trunk of the tree of
life. But, now, take me and you. We more like
branches and limbs.

"Now, you say you saw grapes fall out of the
sky. Maybe so. You saw something and you
acted on what you saw. That's exactly what you
were supposed to do. But the thing you must
remember is this...."

Mr. Taylor set his plate on the nightstand,
placed his hands on his grandson's shoulders,
and looked him in the eyes with a hawkish seri-
ousness.

"When you out on a limb, far away from the
mother trunk, you got to be real careful who you
pick to tell you out on that limb."

Mr. Taylor gulped down some lemonade.

"Your grandma say you met an old man
down by the tracks, say his name was Frank."

"Yes, sir."

"What he look like?"

"He real dark and he got short white hair
and a long wooly beard."

"He tall as me?"

"No way tall as you, Grandpa. Regular
height and kind of stout."

"Say he was from around here? What did he
talk about?"

"Mostly about trains and tracks and places
he been."

"Son, you feel better now?"

"Yes."

"Come on, get up and put some clothes on. Let's take a little walk down by them tracks."

Mike got dressed and he and Mr. Taylor walked toward the front door of the house with their jackets on. Michael carried an umbrella and Mr. Taylor carried his hat.

"Joe Taylor, where you taking that boy this time of night in this kind of weather?"

"The boy's fine, Nettie. Your chicken and biscuits dressed up his stomach real nice. We won't be long. We goin' down by the railroad tracks. I got to see if it's him."

Saying no more, Mrs. Taylor wrapped some fried chicken, biscuits, and a couple of paper napkins in a piece of aluminum foil and carefully stuffed the package into her husband's jacket pocket. Then Mr. Taylor and Mike quietly walked out of the house.

* * * * *

After her husband and grandson stepped into the evening, Mrs. Taylor went into Mike's bedroom and picked up his wet, soiled clothing and took them to the service porch. She opened the lid of the toploading washing machine, set the control knobs, poured powder detergent, and then pushed the water button. As she turned the pockets of Mike's jeans inside out, something small tumbled out. She caught it in the palm of her hand before it fell. It was round, gray-green, translucent, about the size of her thumbnail. She let it roll down her hand. Then

it went away — like an umbrella melting. All
that remained was a small puddle of liquid.
Just as she bent over to inspect the liquid more
closely, she suddenly flung Michael's jeans into
the washing machine along with his other clothing. She closed the lid, wiped her hands dry on
her apron, pulled the light chain, and hurriedly
exited the service porch, making sure the door
was shut tight behind her.

Randy Ross

Conjure

Women

Randy Ross

hen I moved to the Palm Apartments, the only thing new was the building; the only occupants were some old widows who lived in the units on the ground floor. Ginnie rented Number 1. There was Lady Bea in Number 2. Priscilla, she stayed in Number 3, while Miss Lillie occupied Number 4. I just knew they were conjure women. Those gals would sit around that sleek, swaying palm tree in the middle of the courtyard and talk, knit, snack, read, and give folks the eye. They looked at me terribly suspicious when I first got here. After I started givin'em a lot of that good old sweet talk, good-cooking Ginnie loosened up a bit like I was wooing her. Bible-totin' Priscilla would have none of my business, and let me know it real clear. Lady Bea stuttered too much for me to have any kind of probing conversation with her. Miss Lillie was the prettiest one of 'em all. But she never said enough for me to even think about blinking my eye at her. As far as I can calculate, she was the main conjurer. But as long as I was sweet to Ginnie, I was all right with Miss Lillie.

Mrs. Greer, the owner of the apartments, roosts over this place like a hawk. Old people, she said, senior citizens like myself, are the best renters. We generally don't have much income, but our little pension and social security money comes in steady. Besides, we old folks don't go around kicking up a fuss, playing loud music, keeping the neighbors up all night, and messing up the property. Like I said, Mrs. Greer's place is the best kept place around town...for the price. She knows it, she knows that everybody else knows it, and she aims to keep it that way.

So when Mrs. Greer first built this place, she didn't allow no young folks, that is until the day Miss Lillie approached her about it.

"Well, Betty," which is Mrs. Greer's first name, "you know the children are the future, and we've got to prepare the path for them."

"You sure right about that, Lillie, 'cause if somebody don't do something in a hurry, them young'uns go'n tear down everything we done built up."

"Well, Betty, that leads to what I wanted to talk to you about. An old friend of mine from back home...Nettie's her name...her son Donald is coming to Los Angeles, and he's going to need a place to stay. I told Nettie how wonderful your place was and that I would talk to you about one of those vacant units upstairs...."

"Well, Lillie, you know I ain't keen on renting out to young folks; it just ain't worth the trouble.... You sure he want to stay in this part of town? You say it's just him and his son? He never remarried after his wife passed away? Is he all right? Tell him to come by to see me when he gets here; I might have something for him."

* * * * *

When Skipper and his daddy, brother Taylor, moved into Number 11 upstairs, the little fella was knee-high to a grasshopper and quiet as Miss Lillie. Brother Taylor was a real gentleman...got along right fine with the ladies...real respectful with his sprightly "good mornings," crisp "good afternoons," and elegant "good evenings." Whenever he spied the old ladies coming through the front gate with their backs bent over from totin' hefty shopping bags, he'd skip down the twelve steps to give 'em a hand.

Now, the way I saw it, those old gals had little Skipper thinking he could do any old kind of crazy mess. Miss Lillie had him thinking he could fly. I bet he don't know to this day that they're all conjure women.

"Ginnie, wouldn't it be great to be able to fly?"

"Well, Skipper, I don't know. I feel a whole lot better just keeping these bunioned feet of mine right close to mother earth."

"Ginnie, how come people can't fly like birds?"

"See that bluebird yonder?"

"Yes."

"Well, what you see that's different about that bird and yourself?"

"A lot of things. It's blue and I'm brown. It has feathers all over its body and I have hair on my head. It has a pointed beak and I have a mouth with lips and teeth. Our feet are different, too."

"Yeah, but we talkin' about flying. What is it that the bird's got that you don't have that's got to do with flying?"

Little Skipper jumped. "Wings!" he said.

Ginnie beamed and rubbed Skipper on the head. "That's right. We ain't got no wings. And you got to have wings to fly."

"But, Ginnie, my arms are wings, aren't

they?"

"I guess you could say that. But they ain't good enough for flying."

"Why not?"

"'Cause they ain't long enough. And they ain't wide enough."

"Would I be able to fly if I made them longer and wider?"

Ginnie thought a little while. "Well, that depends on how long and wide you make them."

Like me, Miss Lillie had been listening to Ginnie and Skipper all the while. She hardly said much, so when she did talk, everybody listened.

"Son, your body is limited by what your mind tells it it can do. If there's freedom in your mind, your arms can be as wide and long as you want them to be. Wide as the Sahara, long as the Nile. Flight calls for a free mind."

Then Miss Lillie held Skipper's hands between her own.

"Now, repeat after me. Flight is a mind that's free."

And the boy repeated what Miss Lillie asked him to, word for word, looking at Miss Lillie just below her eyes.

*   *   *   *   *

One day not long after Skipper and his daddy moved in, brother Taylor left Skipper in Ginnie's care. Skipper couldn't keep still, so Ginnie let him go play across the street at the park. A while later, he came running back home sniffling, holding his hand tight, while tears cut a narrow trail down his face. He walked slowly over to Ginnie's and put his face against her screen door to look inside. Ginnie was in the kitchen cooking, but Skipper didn't say anything to get her attention. He just looked down at his hand and kept on sniffling. Then he backed away and sat on the steps holding his hand, rocking back and forth trying not to cry.

I was probably the only one who knew what was going on. So I stepped outside to the top of the stairs.

"Skipper, you all right?"

He looked up at me and then down at his hand again without saying a word. So I hobbled down the steps and went over to see what he was trying to show me. That's when I saw the splinter.

"Well, son, it looks like you got a little bit of a problem. Let's see if we can get that splinter taken care of.

"Ginnie! Come on out here and give this young man some help. He done gone and got a great big splinter in his hand."

Ginnie rushed through the screen door gently drying her hands on her apron. She came over to the boy, inspected his hand, and asked him what happened.

"I was playing."

Next thing I know, those old conjure women are coming outdoors and surrounding Skipper. The little fellow's eyes popped wide open. He hardly knew the old ladies, and here they were fussing over him.

"What's the matter, son?" Priscilla cried.

Skipper sniffled and the tears flowed freely down his cheeks.

"Girl, can't...you see the boy done got a long splinter caught...off in his hand," Lady Bea stuttered.

"Yeah, he got a splinter in his hand," Ginnie summarized.

Then Miss Lillie walked out of her apartment and came over to the boy. Everybody got quiet as that old stockbroker commercial. Miss Lillie looked at Skipper's hand, patted it, smiled at his eyes and nodded her head. It was like she was telling him that everything was going to be all right. For the life of me, I just could not understand how Miss Lillie could send messages that way without mumbling a single, solitary word.

Ginnie went inside her apartment and came back with all kinds of stuff: rubbing alcohol, cotton balls, sewing needle. The ladies gathered around Skipper's hand and pushed me out of the way.

When the old ladies started picking at that splinter, little Skipper looked like he was feeling an awful lot of pain. At one point, he hopped like a flea and tried to yank his hand out of that buxom mass of moth balls and talcum powder.

"Be still, son. Be still."

They tugged at his finger and he couldn't get loose; and he couldn't see what the old ladies were doing because their bodies blocked his view. I couldn't even see what was going on in that huddle.

"My, my. This is a pretty bad splinter,"

Priscilla said.

"But it's go'n...come out of there," Lady Bea insisted. Bea crocheted just about everyday, so she probably had the steadiest hand of 'em all. "Ginnie, gi' ...give me that needle."

Soon as Skipper heard the word "needle," he shrieked and tried to yank his arm free again. He cried out loud and pulled hard, but those old gals had his hand locked in a vice.

"Daddy! Ma'Dear!"

"Hush, Skipper, we'll have you fixed up in no time," Ginnie said as she and Lady Bea clamped Skipper's arm between their bodies. Priscilla and Miss Lillie held his hand to keep it from moving. And Lady Bea worked the needle.

Skipper was so scared, looked like his quarter-sized eyes were go'n pop out his head, thinking maybe those old girls were trying to cut his hand off. They held him so tight he couldn't get away. All he could do was bite his lip to keep from hollering.

Then suddenly his arm was free.

Ginnie gathered up her makeshift first aid articles. "Okay, Skipper, your hand is like new. You can go play now. But be careful, you hear?"

The ladies unwrapped Skipper and piled into Ginnie's apartment to confab. Miss Lillie was the last one to go in. Before she let the screen door shut, she smiled at Skipper in that weird, mind-reading way.

Skipper touched the bandage covering his palm and brought his hand up to his nose to sniff the antiseptic smeared underneath. The splinter was gone.

"Looked like they fixed you up, young man."

Skipper smiled and lifted his hand toward me.

"Look'it."

"Yeah, that was a pretty bad splinter you had there."

With a gleam in his eyes, Skipper nodded "yes."

"Did you ever get a splinter when you were a little boy?"

"Sure. Plenty of times."

"Some old ladies helped you, too?"

"I reckon so," I said twice, once for Skipper and the second time for myself.

I started inching my way back upstairs and Skipper got up and hopped about the courtyard, now and again looking through Ginnie's screen door to see what the old ladies were doing.

Then, only God knows the reason, Skipper started jumping from the steps. After the first step, he pressed his face against Ginnie's screen door to see what the old ladies were doing. Two steps up and jump, look through Ginnie's screen, then hop up to the third step, and jump again. Looking through Ginnie's screen, the boy's face beamed. By the time he got to the fourth step, I was back inside my apartment observing through the screen door. When the boy climbed to the fifth step, I just knew he was go'n tear up his little behind. As he sailed toward the ground his feet tipped the bottom step. He limped over to Ginnie's screen in a bit of pain. The ladies were still gossiping and confabbing. Skipper glowed, shook the pain from his legs, and climbed back up to the fifth step. Little biddy fella jumping down all them steps; I was sure he was go'n break up some part of his anatomy.

He squatted down, swung his arms outward and up, sprang forward, flew for the longest short moment, and then squatted back down as he landed. A clapping thud came from his shoes, but he wasn't hurt. Then came the sixth step. I don't think he saw me looking at him, but I saw every little crazy thing he did. I started to open my screen door wide and tell him to get off the steps before he broke his neck. But I didn't.

The boy looked down from the sixth step, fearful but not afraid. He stooped down as far as he could, used the step and the banister to launch himself into the air, his eyes agape. He skidded on the bottom step on the way down, but he hit the ground standing, slightly limping. He hobbled around a bit until he stopped limping, then he walked back up the stairs still not knowing I was watching him. As he set up for another try from the sixth step, I opened my screen door.

"Skipper, get off them steps and go somewhere else to play before you break your back. Come on, tail it out of here. I saw you jump. You made your point. So go on, boy; play somewhere else."

*   *   *   *   *

All was quiet the rest of that day, but the next day Skipper was at it again—climbing and jumping. He started with the low steps for practice then went higher and higher. I shouted out the door at him a few times; told him to stop playing on the steps before he broke his neck. And would you believe those old gray-haired courtyard widows scolded me to leave the boy alone and mind my own business.

After a few days, I got fed up with the mess, walked disgustedly over to Number 11 and rapped on the door with my cane.

Brother Taylor came to the door.

"Hi, Mr. Joe."

"Hey, man, let me in. I got something I want to talk to you about."

"Sure, come on in."

I walked in and, without asking, sat down at the kitchen table where the sun was shining through the open window. That's the way I am. I always look to sit down where there is the most light.

"They tell me you've got a little education, so you should be able to add up the digits I'm about to lay on you."

The young man sat down at the table opposite me and gave me his undivided attention.

"Now, there are four apartment units downstairs, right?"

"Right."

"Now, who lives in those apartments? Old ladies, right?"

"Right."

"How many old ladies live in each apartment? One, right?"

"Right."

"And each of them lives alone, right?"

"I think so."

"They do. Each one of 'em is a widow? Right?"

"I don't know."

"Trust me, they are. Except maybe Lillie ain't never been married. But who knows?"

"Okay."

Then I looked at brother Taylor dead in the eye and asked him, "Now what does that tell you?"

The young man hunched his shoulders as if to say he didn't know what I was getting at.

"Well, if you can't figure it out, I'll tell you. They all conjure women."

The young man stood up from the dinette, went over to the refrigerator and came back with two bottles of cold beer and an opener. He popped the bottle tops, handed me a beer, then sat back down at the table.

"Thank you, brother Taylor." I took a swallow and set the bottle down on the table and looked over at the young man. I think he had a notion what I was getting at. His curiosity got the best of him, so he asked me what I meant by "conjure women."

"Conjure women?" I cried out, running a hand back through my thinning hair. "Roots! Voodoo! Conjure women."

"I see. But why are you telling me this?"

"'Cause they got your boy doing all kinds of craziness outdoors."

"Michael?"

"Yeah, Michael. But everybody calls him Skipper because he's always hopping all over

the place. He thinks he's Tarzan of the jungle
the way he jumps down them steps. I figured he
would have broke up his backside by now, but he
hasn't. Ain't nothing happened at all. Nearly
ten steps he jumped from, and he hit the ground
running and smiling grand."

"Yeah?"

"That's what I'm telling you, son. So what
you think of that?"

"I don't know."

I figured the young man might be able to
latch onto what I was telling him. But he didn't.
For all I know, he might have thought I was
pretty nutty.

"You see what I'm telling you, son?"

"Yeah, Mr. Joe, I see. Who knows? You
may be right."

"Oh, yeah, I'm right all right."

"But there's an aspect to this that should
not be dismissed. Those old ladies have given
Skipper confidence in himself, a new sense of
courage. You know, Mr. Joe, it's okay to take
risks, climb tall trees, jump down the greatest
number of stair steps. It's okay to try to do
things that are out of the ordinary. Indeed, the
pursuit of the extraordinary and the thirst to
know what is unknown but knowable, are what
sustain life's lure."

"That may be all well and good," I say, "but
meanwhile Skipper may break his little ass."

"He'll be all right. The old ladies will make
sure of that."

I thought about the old ladies sitting about
gossiping, knitting, laughing, and Skipper jump-

ing down the steps like they were a serving of peach cobbler.

"Well, son, I hope you're right."

"Whatever happens, Mr. Joe, everything will turn out fine. Michael may not understand it either, but he knows that those old ladies will always be there for him, come hell or high water. Think about it, Mr. Joe. Who's for you? Who's for me? Wouldn't it be great to have somebody watching out for us the way the old ladies watch out for Michael."

"In this here world," I tell him, "you got to watch out for yourself, or you'll wind up dead and gone or down on skid row somewhere living like a sick puppy. It's always been that way. Ain't nothing go'n change it."

I didn't know what else to say to the young man, so I just daydreamed out the window at the passing cars and the green grass that blanketed the park across the street. Then I looked up at the clouds floating around in the sky. They made me think of Miss Lillie. "Flight is a mind that's free," she had told little Skipper. On top of all that, for all I know brother Taylor might have been telling Skipper the same kind of stuff about flying and freedom.

After a couple of beers and spurts of chitchat, it got too quiet around the table. So I reached for my cane.

"Well, I guess I better get on back to the house." I rose from the kitchen table wondering if I had accomplished anything in talking with this young man. "See what I can do about gettin' a little supper together."

"All right, Mr. Joe. Thanks for dropping by. I really enjoyed talking with you."

I opened the screen door into the shadow of a budding mellow evening and hobbled back toward my apartment. Feeling a bit miffed that I didn't get my point across, I looked downstairs toward Ginnie's place. The old conjure women were still sitting around talking in the living room: Ginnie, Priscilla, Lady Bea, and Miss Lillie. Skipper stood alone outside, quiet, pressing his face against Ginnie's screen door, cuffing his eyes with his hands to block the outside light. Just looking. And listening.

When

Are

They

Coming?

Randy Ross

t was still dark outside when Dad pulled the old Ford over to the curb in front of Cheryl's Southern Kitchen. The wind made the outside colder than it looked. Mom rushed to make sure me and my older brother, Jer, had our jackets and stuff for the day. Then she walked us fast to the cafe.

Before we got there, jolly Aunt Cheryl had opened the front door for us. "Well hello there!"

"Good morning, Cheryl," Mom said. "Sorry to hurry, but we're running late for work."

"Honey, don't fret over it."

Mom rushed back to the car. Dad honked the horn twice. Me, Jer, and Aunt Cheryl waved at them as they drove off to work.

Mom usually works five or six days a week and Dad works all the time. Mom works as a secretary for the Department of Water and Power and Dad works in construction. When they stand by each other in the morning, they don't seem to belong together. They look like mismatched shoes. Mom always puts on neat dress clothes, a pretty scarf, high heel shoes, lipstick, and perfume that smells up the house. And Dad wears khaki pants and shirts, old work boots with dirt caked up on 'em, and a hard hat. And he carries a gray metal lunch pail that's shaped like a fat loaf of bread.

When school is out, me and Jer usually stay with Aunt Cheryl. She's my father's sister, but she's a lot older than Dad. Sometimes she acts like she's his mother. She treats almost everybody like she's their mother, even some people who are older than she is. Maybe that's because she doesn't have any children of her own.

Dad is tall and slender, while Aunt Cheryl is short and plump. Sometimes it's hard to believe they're really related. Aunt Cheryl talks up a storm while Dad is pretty quiet. About the only thing they have that's the same is their laugh. They both laugh a lot.

It was early. No one had come to the cafe yet except Miss Claudia. She helped Aunt Cheryl in the kitchen.

"Okay, boys," said Aunt Cheryl, "you know where to put your jackets and belongings."

Me and Jer ran across the linoleum floor toward the family room in the back. I bumped into one of the metal dinette chairs along the way. As usual, Jer got to the room before me. He beats me running because he is more than a year older. If I were seven like him, I bet you I would smoke him in a race.

We put up our jackets, games, books, and toys, then ran back to the cafe and spun on the low, round red padded seats at the counter.

Miss Claudia wore the same lime green dress that Aunt Cheryl wore, and the same huge dark green apron hung from her neck to her knees, and she wore the same thick rubber shoes, the kind that cafeteria workers wear at school. But Miss Claudia was real small for a grown-up. Sometimes when she stood on the other side of Aunt Cheryl, I couldn't even see her.

"Morning," Miss Claudia said.

"Good morning, Miss Claudia," me and Jer

75

said.

"Aunt Cheryl, is Pearl and Basil coming today?" I asked.

"I expect Albert'll be bringing them here before he goes to work."

"Yippee!" I shouted.

Pearl and her younger brother, Basil, are two kids that Aunt Cheryl takes care of a lot. Whenever the four of us are at Aunt Cheryl's together, we usually have fun. Except they all treat me like a stepchild because I'm the youngest one in the group.

The first person to show up for breakfast was a short, old man wearing a cap. A newspaper stuck out of the pocket of his thick wool sports coat. It was Mr. Pratt. He always comes early.

"Good morning, Cheryl, Claudia."

"Good morning," they said.

"Well, look at who we got here today," he said putting his hat on the tall wooden coat pole. "How you young whippersnappers doing?"

"Fine," me and Jer said.

"How's your checker game coming along?" Mr. Pratt asked. He taught me and Jer and Pearl and Basil how to play checkers.

"Fine," we said.

Then Mr. Pratt walked over to the booth he usually sits at and opened his newspaper, and Aunt Cheryl told Jer to take him a cup of coffee.

Jer gets to do more stuff than me around the cafe because Aunt Cheryl says I'm too young. Six is not really that young. I can do just about anything Jer can do. Besides he's only seven years old. So what's the big deal?

"Jer," I said, "you sure took that coffee over to Mr. Pratt real slow. You couldn't go faster than that?"

"Shut up, big head. As if you could do it better."

"I know I can," I said.

"Rockin' Robin, tweet, tweet." That's what Jer says sometimes when he thinks somebody is talking a bunch of baloney.

"Forget you, Jer."

Then I walked over to Mr. Pratt's table and stood there hoping he would ask me to play a game of checkers with him. He smiled at me over the top of his paper. Then he kept on reading. He must have been reading something good, because sometimes he read out loud or laughed out loud.

Since Mr. Pratt was busy, I walked to the counter, sat down, and talked with Aunt Cheryl.

"Aunt Cheryl, you sure Pearl and Basil coming today?"

Aunt Cheryl was cooking up a storm in the kitchen. "I'm as sure as I can be," she said without looking over at me.

I didn't understand how sure that was, but I didn't think it was safe for me to ask her how sure she could be.

"Did they call?" I asked.

"Albert's phone ain't workin'," she said. "Don't fret over it, they'll be here."

I knew she couldn't be all that sure. Because there were times when she said Pearl and

Basil were coming and they never did show up. To me, this time was like those times. Aunt Cheryl said they were coming, but they might not show up.

An old lady wearing a wool overcoat and a dark green hat came into the cafe saying "Good morning" as she took off her coat.

Aunt Cheryl, still cooking up a storm, turned her head. "Hi, Mrs. Winston. I see you're up a little early this morning."

Mrs. Winston hung her coat on the coat pole. "Mornings are meant to be cherished," she said. "The earlier the better. But I done got so old till it's hard for me to get going as early as I used to. I want to get up with the sparrows and the dew. But old Arthur done froze up my old bones so bad that it takes a whole heap of morning just to thaw'em out."

Aunt Cheryl rubbed her neck. "Yeah, child, I know the feeling. When Arthur comes knocking, he loves to stick around and mess with you like a no-good man." And then Aunt Cheryl laughed.

Claudia laughed, too. "Cheryl, you ought to quit it."

Mrs. Winston patted her chest to keep from laughing. "Honey, the truth ain't nothing but the truth. Arthur Itis ain't nothing but a trouble man. But that fella Ben Gay can make you feel so good sometimes that you forget all about Arthur." Then she tapped the floor with her cane and walked slowly over to the cushiony dining booth she always ate in.

I didn't laugh because I didn't understand what they were talking about. Who is Arthur? Why does he mess with people? And why is he no-good? Who is Ben Gay? And what's so good about him? Sometimes grown-ups say weird things that don't make sense. And then they laugh about it. When you ask them what they are laughing about, they say they are not laughing about anything. Jer didn't laugh either. So I guess weird stuff happens to people when they get old.

Then Mr. Pratt folded his newspaper. "Good morning, Mary," he called out to Mrs. Winston.

"Morning, Tom," Mrs. Winston said.

"Everything all right with you?" Mr. Pratt asked.

"Every day is better than the one before," said Mrs. Winston.

"That's what Harvey used to say all the time," said Mr. Pratt. "Yeah, Mary, I certainly do miss him. Your husband sure could play some drafts."

"I most certainly hope so," said Mrs. Winston. "He spent about as much time with them old wooden checkers as he spent with me."

I remember Mr. Winston, too. He was a nice old man with a bald head that was smooth and shiny. He used to rub my head and call me "Sonny Boy." He called Jer "Sonny Boy," too. He even called Dad "Sonny Boy."

Mr. Winston doesn't come around anymore. But now Mrs. Winston comes to Aunt Cheryl's Southern Cafe more than she used to. She always dresses up like she is getting ready to go somewhere special. At first, Mrs. Winston would just sit and have coffee and stare out the window. Then she started taking breakfast. After that she started talking to people about everyday stuff. Then she started talking about Mr. Winston. And the way she talked when she talked about him was so sad that I just knew he wouldn't be coming to Aunt Cheryl's cafe anymore.

When I saw Aunt Cheryl pouring another cup of coffee, I ran to the other side of the counter nearest to the giant metal coffee pot in the kitchen.

"Jer," Aunt Cheryl called, "take this cup of coffee over to Mrs. Winston and be careful not to spill it."

To tell the truth, I'm glad Aunt Cheryl didn't ask me to serve Mrs. Winston. She's the only person I know who eats sunny-side eggs. The way she takes her toast and dips it in the yolk.... Yuk!

I went to see what Mr. Pratt was doing.

"You think Pearl and Basil coming here today?" I asked.

"Who?" Mr. Pratt said.

"Mr. Albert's kids, Pearl and Basil."

"Maybe so," Mr. Pratt said. "That all depends on Albert. If Albert goes to work today, then they're coming."

"Is he going to work today?" I asked.

"That depends on how much hooch he put down last night."

"Hooch?"

Mr. Pratt laughed. "Yeah, son, they'll probably be coming...a man has got to work."

I don't understand everything Mr. Pratt says either. What is hooch? Where did Mr. Albert put it down? And what does it have to do with whether or not Mr. Albert is bringing Pearl and Basil today?

"Set'em up, Pratt!" shouted Mr. Mack as he limped through the door. "It's time for you to meet your master."

Mr. Pratt smiled and rubbed his hands together. "Well, now, look who's come to buy my breakfast." Then looking at me, he said, "Son, go tell your Auntie to fix me my big breakfast this morning."

I ran toward the counter but then stopped and turned around. "Big breakfast?"

"Yeah," Mr. Pratt said, "give it to her like that. She'll know what I'm talking about."

I skipped to the counter to tell Aunt Cheryl what Mr. Pratt said and she laughed and said "Okay."

"Aunt Cheryl, what is a big breakfast?" I asked.

"For Mr. Pratt, that means a thick grilled center-cut pork chop, two soft scrambled eggs, home fried potatoes, with a large serving of apple sauce on the side."

"Aunt Cheryl, how come you let Jer help you, but not me? Can I help out?"

Aunt Cheryl laughed as she reached into the refrigerator for a pork chop. "See if Mr. Pratt and Mr. Mack want coffee."

I skipped to the corner booth where the two

old men always play checkers. The day was brand new and already they were moving red and black wooden pieces across the board.

"Got a sweet little jump for you, brother Mack; hope you like it."

"Well, Pratt, I don't think I'll take that jump; this one over here looks a whole heap sweeter."

"Suit yourself, either way you got to bring it on home."

Mr. Pratt and Mr. Mack moved too fast for me to follow their game.

"King me, brother Mack."

Mr. Mack got real quiet and started thinking hard. That gave me a chance to talk.

"Aunt Cheryl wants to know if y'all want coffee," I said.

"Well, young man," said Mr. Pratt, "I think I'm about ready for another cup. But Mack, here, may not be ready. He's got to figure out a way to get out of that trap I just put him in."

Mr. Mack pointed toward the counter without looking up from the checkerboard. "Go 'head on, son, and get him that coffee. After I turn this trap around, he's going to need it."

I ran to the counter. "One coffee for Mr. Pratt!"

"Coming up," Aunt Cheryl laughed, while putting a hot breakfast plate on the counter.

Jer carried the plate to Mrs. Winston's booth. It had toast and two eggs with the yellow yolk balls bouncing on top.

"Yuk!" I said.

"Boy, shut your face," Aunt Cheryl said,

"and take this coffee to Mr. Pratt."

I got Jer's attention and then I walked fast with the coffee. When I made it back, Mr. Mack was leaning on the table. Mr. Pratt was still waiting for him to make a move.

I put the coffee down by Mr. Pratt. But Mr. Pratt slid the cup over to Mr. Mack's side of the table. I looked at Mr. Pratt and then at Mr. Mack, wondering if I was crazy or something. I was sure Mr. Pratt had asked for the coffee.

"Mack, as slow as you movin' them checkers, you need this coffee more than I do."

Mr. Mack sat up in his seat and reached for the cup of coffee. "Well, brother Pratt, I believe you done cooked my goose this round." Mr. Mack picked up the sugar jar and started pouring lots of sugar into his coffee.

Mr. Pratt smiled. "Now that's the best move you made the whole game, brother Mack. Like I always say, why prolong the suffering? Son, get me another cup of coffee and tell your auntie that Mr. Mack is paying for my breakfast this morning."

When I made it to the counter, Jer was about set to carry another cup of coffee to Mrs. Winston. I bet you the reason she drinks so much coffee is because she needs something strong and hot to keep that gooey egg yolk from sticking on her tongue and teeth. Yuk!

Jer got my attention then whispered, "Watch this." He jogged over to Mrs. Winston's booth with the cup of coffee, put it down real quick, then picked up an empty cup on the way back.

"I bet you can't do that, head," he said.

"I'm getting tired of you calling me 'head,'" I said. "What's that on top of your neck—a sweet pea?"

To be honest, Jer got the coffee to Mrs. Winston faster than I got coffee to Mr. Pratt and Mr. Mack. But like I said, that's just because he's more than a whole year older than me.

"Aunt Cheryl," I said, "I thought Pearl and Basil were coming."

Aunt Cheryl turned some hotcakes on the grill. "Should be here any minute now."

Ms. Claudia walked into the kitchen writing on her order pad. "Cheryl, them kids' daddy is too young and good lookin' to be blanching so sad all the time. What's the matter with him?"

"Albert was a hard working man," Aunt Cheryl said, "till Missie upped and left him and the kids. Now he all messed up—his wife is gone and he don't know the first thing about taking care of children. He brought Pearl and Basil by here one Saturday for ice cream and them kids still had sleep caked up in their eyes. Pearl's hair was tangled up and the hair on that rascal Basil's head looked like peppercorn."

Miss Claudia laughed.

"It was a shame, girl," Aunt Cheryl said. "Pathetic."

I didn't feel like listening to Aunt Cheryl and Ms. Claudia talk about Pearl and Basil and their father, Mr. Albert, so I walked over to where Mr. Pratt and Mr. Mack were sitting.

"Brother Mack," said Mr. Pratt, "I sure wish Harvey Winston was still around to give me some strong competition."

"I don't think you would want Harvey Winston breathing down your neck again," said Mr. Mack. "It was kinda sad the way he used to whip you on this checkerboard."

"And the stuff he did after he knocked you around on the checkerboard was criminal...," said Mr. Pratt.

"...but funny," said Mr. Mack, "that is, if you wasn't the one gettin' whipped."

"Yeah," said Mr. Pratt, "after Harvey beat you, he would get up and play that Charles Brown record on the jukebox and sing along with it. You 'member that?"

"Of course I remember," said Mr. Mack. "Then when the record was over, he would step back to the table smiling and singing."

Mr. Pratt said, "On the 70th day of Christmas, I got from Mr. Mack, three strips of bacon, two cups of coffee, and a big stack of Cheryl's flapjacks."

Then Mr. Mack said, "On the 71st day of Christmas, I got from Mr. Pratt, bacon, coffee, flapjacks, and a porterhouse on top of that."

Mr. Pratt and Mr. Mack laughed real hard. But I don't know why they laughed. I didn't see anything all that funny about what they said.

"Yeah, that Harvey Winston was too much," said Mr. Pratt, "but my pockets don't miss him none."

Just more weird stuff that old people say. I sure hope Mom and Dad don't start saying a lot of weird stuff when they get old.

"Well, brother Mack, since you footin' my breakfast, I suppose I can spare a little change to put some music into this place." Mr. Pratt walked slowly over to the arch-headed jukebox and slid some coins down the slot.

"Brother Pratt," said Mr. Mack, "would you be so kind to play that Charles Brown record for me?"

"Why you want to hear that? Long time 'fo Christmas come again."

"'Cause that was the last checker game you go'n beat me till after Christmas."

Mr. Pratt laughed and pushed some buttons on the jukebox and the record started playing. "Merry Christmas, Baby...."

When the music came on, Mrs. Winston bowed her head, then got up and walked to the coat pole. Mr. Pratt helped her with her coat. I don't think she liked music for breakfast. At least not that song.

"Good day," said Mrs. Winston.

"See you the morrow," Aunt Cheryl said from the kitchen.

"Bye, Mary," said Mr. Pratt.

Before she walked through the front door, Mrs. Winston called Jer over. "Here's a quarter, young man, for the extra fast service you provided today; you're some kind of hard worker. But the next time you bring me my coffee, slow down a little bit. I would much rather have a slow-coming whole cup of coffee than a fast-coming one that's only filled half way and rocking like a wave in the ocean."

"Yes, ma'am."

Mrs. Winston closed the front door and the bells jingled.

"Aunt Cheryl," I said, "when Pearl and Basil coming?"

"I don't know what's keepin' those children," Aunt Pearl fretted.

"Maybe Mr. Albert got up late again," I said.

"I'll be glad when they get here." Jer slurped a spoonful of Cheerios and sweet milk. "Then maybe I'll have some fun."

"Me, too," I said, "'cause I don't like to listen to you slurp on milk like you're eating hot soup or something."

"You act like you don't slurp."

"I don't slurp as loud as you. When you slurp, the front window shakes."

Jer squinted his eyes and then got up from the metal dinette, picked up his bowl of cereal, and walked toward the front of the cafe. Then he stirred his cereal, lifted a spoonful toward his lips, slurped as loud as he could, then perked his ears toward the large front glass pane.

"Boy, what in the world are you doing making all that noise?" shouted Aunt Cheryl, walking out of the kitchen. She had been busy fixing breakfast for a few customers sitting at the counter. "If you don't get yo' hindpa'ts over to the table with that cereal...."

Jer scampered back to his seat. "I didn't hear a sound, stupid."

"Maybe you didn't have enough milk," I said. "Or maybe your spoon is not big enough."

"Forget you, you big head clown."

"Mack," said Mr. Pratt, "you hear about that fire last night?"

Mr. Mack took a sip of coffee. His slurp was as loud as Jer's. "Where?"

"Southside."

"What got burned?"

"One of them old wood-framed houses."

Mr. Mack laughed. "Them old houses on Southside ain't no count."

"Clang!" A big, black skillet dropped on one of the eight burners on the stove. Aunt Cheryl was shaking.

"Anybody get hurt?" Mr. Mack asked.

"Maybe so. They had all kinds of sirens round 'bout."

Aunt Cheryl wiped her hands on her apron and sat down at the table with me and Jer and just looked down at the table like she was looking through it. But she could not have been looking through it, because the table was made of metal.

I kept eating my cereal and looking at Aunt Cheryl. Jer did the same thing. I looked at Jer and he looked at me. I guess he felt, like me, that something was wrong with Aunt Cheryl. She wasn't her everyday self. Then she raised up and stared out the window. But from the way her eyes looked, I don't think she could see anything.

"Mack," said Aunt Cheryl, "I need you to take me somewhere."

"Sure."

"Where you going, Aunt Cheryl?" I said.

"Y'all stay here with Claudia and Mr. Pratt, hear. Claudia, take over the kitchen. Mr. Pratt, watch over them boys for me. We'll be right back."

"Sho' thing, Cheryl," said Mr. Pratt.

Aunt Cheryl didn't come right back. When an old man sitting alone at a booth left, me and Jer stopped playing and stood looking out the window, wondering when Aunt Cheryl was coming. Besides it was boring. Usually, we had Pearl and Basil to mix it up with. But they hadn't come yet.

About an hour after Aunt Cheryl and Mr. Mack left, Mr. Pratt started getting fussy. He walked over to the window and looked out with us.

"Boys, Cheryl said she was coming right back, or I done got so old I ain't hearing things right. I done finished reading the newspaper, so I know they shoulda been here by now."

Me and Jer didn't say anything to Mr. Pratt; we just kept looking through the window waiting for Aunt Cheryl.

"Doggone women," Mr. Pratt said, "...tell you one thing, and it always end up being something else."

Me and Jer kept standing at the window waiting for Mr. Mack's big Oldsmobile to pull up to the curb.

When Aunt Cheryl and Mr. Mack finally made it back, a lot more than an hour had passed. But when I saw the looks on their faces, especially Aunt Cheryl's, I sort of wished they were still gone. They looked terrible. Aunt Cheryl looked like she had been crying. Her eyes were red and puffy.

"What took y'all so long, Mack?" Mr. Pratt asked.

Mr. Mack sat down at the counter and kept to himself.

Mr. Pratt went over and sat by Mr. Mack at the counter.

"What took y'all so long?"

Mr. Mack spoke almost in a whisper. "Albert Broadnax."

"What about him?" said Mr. Pratt.

"He dead."

Mr. Pratt looked stunned. "Dead? Dead how?"

"That was his house that caught 'fire last night."

"Well, I'll be."

"What about Pearl and Basil?" Jer asked.

"Who?" snapped Mr. Mack.

"Pearl and Basil," Jer repeated, "Mr. Albert's kids."

"Yeah," I said, "where are they?"

Aunt Cheryl's face twisted up. Her body started jerking and the table she sat at started shaking.

Mr. Mack took off his hat and shook his head from side to side.

Miss Claudia came out of the kitchen and stood behind the counter. "What's the matter, Mack?"

Mr. Mack raised his head and looked at

Claudia. He looked at Aunt Cheryl, who was still moaning at the table. Then he stared through the cafe window.

"They got burnt up. Everybody dead. Broadnax and both his kids."

The cafe turned quiet as sleep. Except Aunt Cheryl started crying and shaking more than before.

I really didn't like seeing Aunt Cheryl sad that way, so I told what I knew.

"Pearl and Basil ain't dead," I said.

Aunt Cheryl looked at me kind of screwy— like she hated me and felt sorry for me at the same time.

Jer pulled me out of the cafe back to the family room.

"Why you go and say that, stupid?"

"Say what?"

"Why you say they not dead?"

"'Cause we just saw them last night."

"Yeah, but this is another day."

"I know."

"So, anything coulda happened since last night."

"Yeah, but they couldn'a died that quick."

Jer started shouting and tears were coming down his face.

"What are you talkin' about? Something that's alive can die just like that. Just like when you step on a cockroach or hit a fly with a swatter. They're all smashed up, they don't move no more, they don't make sounds, they dead...."

"Yeah, but Pearl and Basil didn't die just like that."

"How do you know?"

"'Cause I know," I said.

Jer slapped my head. "Yeah, you know all right."

I pushed him back. He slapped at my head again, I ducked under the slap and slapped at his head. Then he tackled me and got me in a headlock. We wrestled, made a lot of noise, and shouted at each other.

"Let me go, Jer."

"If you stop being stupid, stupid."

"You better let me go."

I wrestled Jer on the sofa and then we fell on the floor and knocked over a lamp on the coffee table.

"Y'all come out of that room and go outdoors and play!"

Me and Jer froze on the floor. Aunt Cheryl was serious. We got up and walked real quiet through the cafe. I looked over at Aunt Cheryl as we passed, but she didn't look at us. She was all to herself. We went out the front door real quiet and sat on the steps.

"Jer?" I said.

"What?"

"When are Pearl and Basil coming?"

Randy Ross

Robbie

the

Genie

Randy Ross

have sulked in this magical goose-necked jar so many years now that I am certain my predecessor, Mr. Singbe, duped me into taking over this timeless abode.

The last time I saw Singbe the allied forces huddled in Versailles to extract reparations from the vanquished German warmongers. That was the summer of 1919.

"Robbie, man," he had said with glee, "genieland is a portal to eternity, absolutely unconstrained by encumbrances that fetter your earthly domain. There exist no walls, zillions of geniettes, and endless hours, years, eons of risk-free fun. Total bliss, man. And I have sixty good years to show for it. Look at me. Do not this old Mandingo look good?

"So may I humbly render a modest suggestion for your consideration? Don't waste your third solicitation on that which is mundane. What you know as life is but a gnat's eye on the Milky Way of time. To request a wish that is bound by your world truly would be profligate or simply unthinking. Wish for eternity, man, and the wish is yours."

Having gotten to know Singbe during lengthy negotiations over a few other wishes, I suspected he could read my thoughts.

"Why, you are thinking, am I so eager to offer you this priceless gift? It's simple, man. Your next wish will be your last; after you have had it I will be free."

"Now you are talking above my head, Mr. Singbe. What is genieland if it isn't freedom?

You do what well pleases you. You work your own hours with no chance of being fired. And for compensation, you are rewarded with eternal fun."

"You think very well, man. What explanation could I offer you but that I wish to be freed from eternity. Perhaps you think it unwise, but that is my choice. Had you been negotiated from your motherland, manacled and stuffed in the hold of an ocean schooner like a can of sardines, then perhaps you would grasp my choice."

"But Mr. Singbe," I said, "freedom from the jar means mortality."

"Precisely. Freedom to live as Mandingo and freedom to die as Mandingo. I AM Mandingo!"

Eventually, Singbe had me so rapt in his webbed logic, I uttered "yes" to his offer of eternity—though with extraordinary vexation. But "yes" is "yes" in the protocol of genieland. In a puff, I was spiraling recklessly down the curved neck of the bottomless jar, seemingly accelerating each mile of the way. On my descent, I formed truly sinful combinations of profane words for Singbe but was too shocked to get them out of my mouth. Had Singbe and his fellow African captives not mutinied the Amistad, he never would have come upon the magical jar stashed with the doubloon in the slain captain's trunk. And I, of course, would not be in my present predicament.

A zillion thoughts crammed my brain as I tumbled in the jar. Who is this genie who calls himself Singbe? Did he really expect me to be-

lieve that an ex-president of the United States
helped to defend him in the highest court in the
land against the capital charges of mutiny and
murder? Maybe the genie really was not Singbe.
If not, then who was he? Could he have been the
lowly enslaved cabin boy, Antonio, who had con-
veyed to Singbe and his fellow captives that they
were going to be eaten by the whites? In that
case, a perpetual tumble in the jar might have
been harsh punishment for whatever moral
shortcomings he may have had. I, myself, am
neither perfect in intellect nor morals by any
stretch of judgment. But my shortcomings and
excesses surely were insufficient to warrant my
submission to this unjust treatment. Yet, down
the jar I plunged at warp speed, out of control,
ignorant of my destination or even if I had one.
I imagined the eerie possibility that the genie
who had lured me into the jar was really a de-
mon to whom I had granted my soul and now
who had me tumbling rapidly toward a dungeon
of fire in which I would burn forever.

Several days passed, but the bottom of the
jar was still not in sight. Eventually thoughts of
hell and burning and "Who's Singbe?" stepped
out of my head. I began to focus more sharply on
my state of being.

"Who am I?"

Sound again blared from my mouth.

"Where am I?"

But it was not the voice I had known; the
voice squeaked regrettably like glass on a chalk-
board.

"Why am I tumbling down the jar?"

The high-pitched echoes emanating from my throat bounced around in the jar like a brood of rodents fussing over a morsel.

Wanting not to hear my voice again, I kept quiet and confined myself to contemplation. I began to think about how I might smooth my descent. After many hours I learned to slide down on my back, feet first. Then I learned to slide down with my legs crossed and hands clasped behind my head, much like swaying on a hammock. Eventually I got the hang of it and promptly fell asleep like a tot for the first time in how many days I cannot say.

Many days passed before I came upon the critical insight that while I was being moved along at warp speed I, personally, had not moved one inch. So I stood up and began moving about with the awkwardness of an infant taking his first steps. Thereafter, life in the jar became a bit more interesting.

For the first few years, this place was precisely what Singbe had made it out to be — endless hours of risk-free fun. As I learned to move about, I explored other sectors of genieland. Occasionally, I met another genie or geniette. But I never talked to any of them, nor they to me. At least, not using sound. I suspect, like me, their voices had been quieted by those aggravating high-pitched echoes. Besides, genieland was home to genies from all over the world's space and time. Even if we wanted to talk, how would we have been able to understand each other? When possible, we looked each other in the eye, used sign language, or touched. With some occupants, the complications were so great, it just didn't seem worth the trouble to attempt communication.

All in all, genieland is a stupendous nerve center of maddening bliss. There exists no official government that regulates oddities. Everybody does his own thing. But strangely enough, the unbelievable disorganization in this place works astonishingly well for at least three reasons: everybody is free; existence is eternal; and property rights are not an issue. Genieland doesn't belong to me; neither does it belong to the others; we belong to genieland.

Then, of course, there is airswirling — arguably the one distinction of genieland that softened my intolerance for anarchy. At the peak of my first airswirl with a manic geniette, I was prepared to bow down and kiss Singbe's huge, dark callused feet. It is difficult to explain, but imagine, if you will, the quality of an orgasm attained while coupling with a swinging Josephine Baker inside a truck tire spinning at warp speed. The climbing orgasm struggles to erupt but cannot; it remains locked in the airswirl. From all I have learned over my decades in the jar, this has to be the most dangerous activity in genieland. But the worst that ever comes of it is excruciating nausea that ebbs in a short while. On Earth, by contrast, airswirling would have meant instant heart failure.

Most genies I met had become hooked on airswirling. I, too, was on the titillating path of addiction. But after my umpteenth experience, airswirling had begun to drag on me. The act

Randy Ross

had become too predictable, too routine. Every peck of time after my second year in genieland — between eating olives and smooching with geniettes — I became increasingly bored and hence angry. Surely, if ever I caught up with Singbe, a war would commence. Or perhaps I would trick him into airswirling on Earth. But I have neither seen nor heard from Singbe since the day I said "yes" to his offer of eternity. Given his tenacity, I suspect he made it back to the land of his youth and there faced with courage his mortality.

* * * * *

Decades of boredom had laid me open to serious bouts of depression. To shuck off my rut, I began to jog a lot. Indeed, running became more important than eating and grooming. Gradually, I lost a lot of weight and grew a mustache and beard. As my body whittled down, some of the beautiful geniettes with whom I used to airswirl came to disavow me. But, at that moment, the jilting did not faze me, for jogging had subdued my appetite for airswirling.

Around my fiftieth year of timeless, risk-free ennui, a fascinating thing happened: the jar spun and shook. It felt like a heavenly earthquake; the closest thing to danger I had known in decades.

As if by instinct, I swished toward and through the curved neck of the magical jar and puffed out of its opening. A skinny little almond complexioned kid stood below looking up at me in pop-eyed awe. The magical jar lay near his

100

feet on the floor of a dark, moldy cellar. I had not talked for half a century, so I was eager to try. But the kid seemed afraid, so I didn't say anything. I calmly looked about the cellar from one corner to the other. Spider webs threaded the wire spokes of the wheels on an old bicycle whose faded streamers sagged from rubber handle bars. Dusty storage boxes were stacked along the walls, some covered with crinkly aqua blue plastic covering. A paper kite leaned against a lawn mower. Tinted Mason jars filled with preserves neatly lined an opened cupboard.

"Who are you?" the young boy blurted aghast.

"The name's Robaire, but you may call me Robbie."

"But you came out of that jar. How did you do that?"

I feigned astonishment. "You really saw me come out of a jar?"

"Yeah."

"Do you really believe I came out of that jar?"

"I don't know."

"How could I have come out of a jar?"

"Maybe you're a genie."

I had been acting on the assumption the kid had no idea what a genie was. Up to now I had avoided the issue because I feared he might panic and run away, leaving me no choice but to return to the jar.

"So you've heard of genies, have you?"

"Yeah, I read about them in school?"

"You don't say?"

"Yeah, you rub the magic bottle and a big bald-head genie with an earring in one ear comes out in a puff of smoke and says in a real deep voice, 'Yes, Master, your wish is my command.'"

"How interesting." I was concerned because I looked nothing like this kid's idea of a genie.

"So then you ain't a genie," the kid concluded.

"Why do you say that?"

"You're too skinny to be a genie."

I looked down at my body to validate the kid's observations.

"You ain't bald-headed and you don't wear no earring."

"True."

"And you look too young to be a genie."

"Thanks for the compliment."

"And genies don't wear clothes like that."

I looked down at my seamless sneakers, cotton jogging suit, and then fingered my Brooklyn Dodgers baseball cap.

The kid's eyes dilated and he raised his voice. "And genies don't wear sunglasses!"

"You're probably right."

"So if you ain't a genie, you must be...a burglar!"

Before I could get his attention, the kid had darted out of the cellar. I had no choice but to return to the jar. There was calm. Days, weeks, months passed. Then years. The calm began to shoot my nerves to pieces. Would the kid's curiosity move him to invoke my presence again? When?

I resolved that when he called again—if ever he would—my facade and demeanor would be apropos. I shaved my head and mustache, ate lots of spaghetti to put on the pounds, pierced my ear and threaded it with an over-sized virtually pure gold earring, and I started doing everything, from jogging to airswirling, wearing togas and sandals.

I twiddled my fingers nearly twenty years before the kid beckoned me again. As I puffed out of the jar, my expression no doubt revealed my vexation over how much time had elapsed since our introduction in the cellar. But I was primed to put on a sparkling performance. I sat in the air in an Indian squat suffering all the trappings of a genie as he knew them.

"Young master, your wish is my command."

So what does the kid say?

"Come on, Robbie, why don't you drop that genie routine. First of all, I ain't your master or nobody else's; that's leftover bullshit from slavery. So don't call me 'master.' My name is Marquette."

I nodded in the affirmative.

"Second of all, you know that I know you ain't no genie.... And I ain't scared of you no more either."

The kid, or young man, was now older than me, at least in Earth years. He stood alone in a dark place. But it was not the old damp cellar.

I lowered myself to the floor. "Were you afraid of me before?"

"You damn straight. There was nobody in that cellar but me. When the police came to see

if the burglar was still in the cellar, you were
gone, but the jar was still there. The top was
back on it, and I didn't put it there. So I took the
jar with me and hid it and didn't say nothing to
nobody. Can you picture what would have happened if I had said something? One thing for
sure, I woulda been in an institution long before
now.

"Institution?"

"Yeah, Camarillo, or some other place for
crazy people."

"Are you in an institution now?"

"Of course, can't you tell?"

"The thought hadn't crossed my mind."

"What do you think those bars are for?"

I looked about the dim room and spied the
long metal bars. A stained open toilet protruded
in the back of the small room, and a small bed
with a frail mattress was pressed against the
off-white wall on one side, while makeshift cabi-
nets lined the other.

"So how did you end up in a room with
bars?"

"Forgery."

"Forgery?"

"Yeah, I lost my job, ran out of money, lost
my home, my wife, and my car. So I wrote somebody else's name on some checks. I got a lot of
money...and a lot of time."

"You should have called me."

"That's exactly what I was thinking."

I rubbed my hands with delight. "Well,
shall we get started?"

Then the twerp held up the jar and said, "A

little later; I just wanted to make sure you were real."

"I am quite real. Now about those wishes...."

"I don't have any wishes yet. But I got a couple of months to think about them before I get out on parole. So I will definitely be getting back to you, my man...in the drop of a hat."

"As you wish," I lamented.

"By the way, Robbie, whatever happened to your cap?"

"Which one?"

"The Brooklyn Dodgers baseball hat? I bet you that cap's worth a mint these days."

"I lost it while airswirling."

"Airswirling? What is airswirling?"

"It's difficult to explain." Gloomily I began evaporating back into the jar. "If you like, I will explain it the next time you call on me."

*   *   *   *   *

The jar shook. The young man was calling again. Over a period of nearly three years, I had granted him two wishes: one predictable, one curious.

I figured I would let him sweat a bit to give him a dose of how it feels to be kept waiting so long. Then his palms rubbed the sides of the jar furiously causing a summer rain. I jumped up angrily and popped out of the jar.

"Hey, Robbie. Why are you dripping wet? Looks like you got hit with a big bucket of water at the end of a championship football game."

My cottony jumpsuit was soaked from head

to toe.

"We were hit with an unexpected storm just before I came up."

"Gee, you look a lot more trim."

"More fruit, less spaghetti, more airswirling."

"Is airswirling as great as you say it is?"

"Indescribably intoxicating. Without a doubt, you, I'm sure, would never get your fill."

Marquette towered over me bereft of the wonder, hunger, and hopelessness his eyes had registered when my stupendous figure had mushroomed above the magical jar the day he had invoked me from prison.

"Well, Robbie, it's been rough coming up with that third wish. But I've thought about it long and hard. Eternity, the way you described it to me, sounds great. I have had many dreams about airswirling.... Maybe you could arrange for me to try it out in advance; you know, a little sample."

"Don't even think of it. You would not survive the experience on Earth. But in genieland? Well, anything is possible. Of course, you know how you can get to genieland."

"The way you keep rubbing it in, how can I forget. But, quite frankly, eternity ain't my bag. It's too me, me, me. I have already been too selfish with my first two wishes. Ever since I won my lawsuit against the police department, 'How much?' is a question I will never have to ask again. While I have shared a tad of my good fortune with folks, friends, and even a few strangers, I personally have been livin' extra

large for the past couple of years. But what I
don't understand, Robbie, is why when I asked
you to make me a millionaire for life, you went
back into the jar. Then when I called you back
out again, you told me that if I ever got into trouble that I should stop for nobody or nothing until
I got to a specific location. So when the police
started tailing me that morning, the only thing
I thought about was how to get to that spot before my car came to a stop. When I finally got
there, the police were so mad at my black ass
they beat me half to death. I had no idea, and
did not care at that moment, that someone
nearby had whipped out a brand new VCR and
filmed the police pouncing on me with their
sticks, feet, and shocking me with their electri-
cal fishing rod. Quite frankly, Robbie, I don't
understand why it had to go down that way."

"Well, there is more than one way to skin a
cat," I explained. "First you need to understand
that everybody asks for wealth. But what most
people don't understand is that finding wealth
for someone without creating suspicion is not
easy. You cannot imagine the depth of thought
that went into that plan."

"So why didn't you tell me what the plan
was?"

"Had I told you what was going to happen,
would you have tried to get there?"

"Do I look like an idiot?"

"That is precisely the point."

"How come you couldn't just let me win the
California Lottery and be done with it?"

"Well, I thought about that. But after considering all the permutations and risks, I decided against it. First, I would have had to find out what numbers the millions of other players had, because in order to insure you a lifetime of wealth, I would have had to make certain you were the sole winner; if the pot were split between you and other winners, I might be in sort of a jam."

"Yeah, but you could have easily set up another lottery."

"That would have been too obvious. The likelihood of someone winning the California Lottery twice in a lifetime is over a trillion to one. Everyone from psychics to the FBI would be tagging you, one group wondering if you had some sort of special powers and the other trying to figure out how you rigged the game. Believe me, if those wackos ever got on your tail, you would come to hate me for the rest of your life.

"Speaking of life, Marquette, I still strongly suggest that you consider my offer of eternity for your third wish."

"Well, Robbie, I guess what I'm trying to say is that I don't trust you."

"Who do you trust?" I shouted. "But that's beside the point."

"No it is not beside the point. Take my second wish. It was so simple, yet you even conned me on that one. Sure, Whitney has been singing to me nightly. I no longer feel depressed and I am sleeping well again. Just like a baby. But it's all smoke and mirrors. I think Whitney is with me, but she really isn't. You laid some sort of high-tech holography on me. It seems so real that I haven't really nailed it down yet. Then perhaps you say, 'So what's the problem, you asked for it, you got it.' You may be right. After all, if Whitney sang me to sleep every night in the flesh, by now Bobby would be a nerve-wracked insomniac, just as I had been.

"But eternity? I don't think I'm cut out for it. But thanks for being so considerate. And thanks for the Whitney hologram. And a special thanks for cooking up that ingenious make-me -or-break-me plan that, well, broke me before it made me. I just want to thank you a bunch for looking out for me, because, Robbie, my man, you are one hell of a dude."

I dunked an olive into a martini while bobbing on a floater in the heated pool of Marquette's sprawling hilltop estate, and took deep breaths to keep from overreacting to the twerp's sarcasm.

"By the way, Robbie, have you ever stood still long enough to listen to Whitney sing? Compared to Whitney, birds sing like shit."

"Then what shall be your third wish?"

"It's simple. I wish there was no more racism in the world."

"Hmmm," I sighed, stirring my martini with an index finger. "Are you sure that's what you want?"

"Absolutely, unequivocally, without a doubt. In your own words, Robbie, what greater gift could a man bestow upon the world?"

Now he was mocking me. Wealth and infamy had transformed Marquette into an asshole. But I am a genie. I had puffed out of the jar on my own accord and thus was bound to granting him three wishes. My feelings and emotions had to be cast aside, else all I had done for the ingrate to this point would be nullified. What a terrible thought.

"Marquette, racism has many faces and definitions. For example, racism may refer to an individual's hatred of others because of their race. Or it may refer more generally to discrimination on the basis of race."

"Either or both. It's all bad, Robbie. And it's got to end. We have all got to find a better way to get along."

I extended my arms as far as I could. "Do you wish to eliminate racism throughout the entire world?"

"Of course. Is that a problem for you?"

"Well, the world is far more expansive than you think. Over five billion living people reside on this planet today, and billions have come and gone before you."

"What I'm asking you is, is that a problem? Is the wish too big for you to handle? I really like you because you're cool, but you're not the only genie in the world, you know."

"The only reason you know that is because I told you," I blared angrily. "But that's beside the point."

"So what is the point, Robbie?"

"The point is that you're asking me to do something so big, so stupendous that God, himself, hasn't worked out the answer."

"You may be right, Robbie. So let's keep it simple. I wish that racism be removed from

Southern California, especially Los Angeles. That should not be such a tall order? If it is, let me know, so we can deal with it. All I'm asking is that you wipe the racial slate clean. Is that okay?"

I knew Marquette really didn't know what he was asking for, but quite frankly at that moment I didn't give a damn. I wanted out of the jar. I was bored to wit's end. Freedom from the jar was so close I could smell it. I was willing to do almost anything to get out.

In the way of the genie the young man had seen the first time he had called me from that shadowy, dank prison cell, I floated above the heated pool and sat in the air with my legs crossed. Then I snapped the fingers on both my hands.

"Master, your wish is my command."

* * * * *

I slapped my face hard. Smarting from the needle-like sting, I concluded that I had succeeded in becoming a man again. Free at last!

Cottony, steamy clouds tossed about gaily in an endless clear, blue sky. A bald eagle glided low without choking on smog or losing its bearing.

I looked about the land satisfied that I had fulfilled the conditions for my exit from the magical jar. But unlike most genies who had sought freedom from genieland (and only a few ever want to leave), I lacked the hearty, contemptuous laugh that ordinarily accompanies the moment of freedom.

Highways? There were none. No Fords, Chevies, or extemporaneous skateboards. The smell of crude oil filled the basin, but a gas station was not to be found. No trains, no tracks. No houses and no squatters. I had had to go a long way back to get to a time when racism did not scour the land.

In a place that would have been 1st and Grand, that would have been the Los Angeles Superior Court, pintos lapped water from a small, crooked stream.

Several miles northwest, in a desolate place that would have been Simi Valley, huge black ants taxied a stilled grasshopper to their lair, and a hyena yanked on a buffalo's carcass as a strong wind blew tumbleweeds over the barren land.

No babies cried. There were no voices, no radios, no children playing four-square or tetherball in the school yard. No voices!

A dust-toting wind tickled majestic trees and caused a grainy whistle. And the largest tree—it was a redwood—had been where the Foothill police station would have been. It was bent over and oozing sap at the break in its trunk, having been whacked by a bolt of lightening.

Again I was a man, imbued with the awful fear of taking on Earth's impossible, yet magnificent, game of granting the living but a long moment to carve a niche in time. Yet I was excruciatingly troubled by what I saw. Laughter escaped me. I was free, but I choked with the feelings and insecurities of a man. Tears streamed from my eyes. My vocal cords vibrated and suddenly my voice screamed out of me over the land. The animals paused. The clouds stood still.

My emotions had gotten the best of me. Too bad. In effect, I had vitiated the wish I had granted Marquette. In a flash of lightening I was tumbling down the maple-colored neck of the magical jar from which I had just emerged after over seventy years.

So here I go again—quiet shadows, no walls, and airswirling with lukewarm, high strung geniettes. In twenty years, maybe thirty, I am certain another innocent dreamer shall come along to spin, rub, shake the jar with vigor. When that happens, this time perhaps I will be graced with an unbending courage to chance the passionate, whimsical dance of mortality.

Randy Ross

Run

Low

Randy Ross

he scraggly crater-like scar that snaked his neck evoked memories of that frightful day thirty years ago. When the bullets flew, everybody ran. Except Bo.

* * * * *

Hordes of teenage spectators packed the wooden bleachers awaiting the ultimate race of the final meet of the track season, wondering who would be crowned the fastest runner of Central Junior High School. There is nothing more exhilarating than a race. Foot races create a glorious tension in the pit of the soul. "Suped-up" motor bikes, funny cars, and supersonic jets yield to the drama of the human body propelling itself forward, seducing its feet to rebel against gravity.

The head official announced on the bullhorn that the senior 100-yard dash was next. The eight fastest runners in the school, representing as many intramural teams, lined up. Bo Williams, a week away from graduating from Central, was the one to beat. His sneakers were expected to sweep dust into the eyes of his opposition and, as legend had it, skid into the tenth grade at W. E. B. Du Bois High.

"Runners take your marks. Set. Pow!" The runners came out low. Except Bo. Bo lacked tolerance for "good" running technique, and advice ran off him like water off an umbrella. The purpose of racing is to get there first. So long as he kept winning, technique seemed irrelevant.

When the smoke from the starter's pistol cleared, the race was half over. Bo, running straight and high, breathed down the neck of little Benny Ford, who, as usual, had burst from the blocks with his patented flying start. The crowd roared as Bo passed him and took over the lead.

Little Stevie Roe, running a respectable fourth, gritted his teeth in pursuit. He had been trying to catch Bo since the two were kids. At first Stevie had run last against all the kids. His embarrassment was cushioned by the knowledge that the faster runner, Bo, was also his best friend. Stevie figured that he and Bo were a good team since Bo had the front end covered while he covered up the rear. Stevie marveled at Bo's running. He would start out standing straight and he would finish standing straight. Never saying much, he would stand at the starting line and look intently ahead to the finish line. While the other kids raced for the fun of it, Bo was always serious and determined. And usually he won. When he did, he did not jump up and hoot and holler. He simply smiled while the others tried to figure out how he could run so fast. Perhaps he ran fast because he feared losing. Once, he felt so bad about losing a foot race that he left the park immediately, silently dejected, his head bowed, his hands stuffed in the pockets of his blue jeans.

But that was then. While he still ran straight and high, and disdained earthly technique, the final race of Central Junior High's track season easily belonged to Bo. As he crossed the tape, he raised a clenched fist in victory, peered over at the roaring crowd spilling out of the old splintery wooden bleachers onto the asphalt, and shouted one word. "Yes."

*   *   *   *   *

The school bell rang for the last time that Friday. Stevie showered, dressed, picked over books and materials for weekend homework, closed his gym locker and, out of habit, spun the cylinder on his combination lock. Per custom, he sauntered three rows down to check on Bo.

"How come you run so fast and dress so slow?"

Bo stood in front of his locker methodically buttoning his shirt. It was as if he were savoring his victory to the last drop of evaporating sweat.

"What's the rush, brother Roe?"

"There are only so many minutes of sunlight in a day, homey. And I want to get as many of 'em as I can. Somebody else can have the night."

"Well, if you don't worry yourself about time," Bo said, "she won't mess with you."

"Yeah, right. Come on, man, let's get out of here. You beat me in the race today, but let's see if you can double up on some hoops."

Most days, after-school seemed much more energetic than before-school. There's that extra bounce in the adolescent strut. First the boys would go home, have a snack, maybe do a little homework, then meet up at the park to play basketball into evening.

With Stevie at his side, Bo exited Central

Junior High's main entrance with a glow about him. The principal and physical education teachers monitored a crowd lingering about the front of the school.

Two boys from 68th Street elementary school had waited around to get a close look at Bo. "Look! There he is!" Bo smiled and waved at them.

Then a confident yet delicate voice came from behind.

"Hi, Bo. You ran a great race."

"Thanks," Bo said.

It was Angela Caruthers, Central's smart but cute student body president. Stevie had gotten to know her well through student government. There he had sat as a knight at Angie's round table and eventually fallen in love with her fine diction and bleached smile. But he had never told her about his feelings. All of their verbal exchanges had been governed by Robert's Rules of Order.

"Point of clarification, Madam President," said Stevie.

"What?"

"Bo wasn't the only one in the race...."

A few blocks down Central Avenue, Stevie and Bo ran into Brian Lanier, who was slow-walking with four of his running buddies from the public housing project across the tracks. Brian's uncle Blue coached basketball at the park. Stevie knew two of the guys from school. The others were strangers. But that was not unusual. Everybody who was somebody always attended the final meet of Central Junior High's track season.

As he and Bo caught up to the pack, Stevie called out, "Hey, what's happ'nin', Brian?"

"What's goin' on, Stevie," Brian said as he looked northward to Slauson Ave. "Hey, Bo, sweet race, man."

"Thanks."

"Say, what about me?" Stevie said. "Didn't I run a good race? Man, if I hadn'a slipped out of the blocks, I woulda been breathing down Bo's neck."

"Bologna," said Bo, causing Stevie and Brian to laugh heartily.

Stevie kept up the chit-chat with Brian and got a few laughs. But only from Brian. Bo and the other guys wore tight faces and seemed unmindful of the light banter.

Something ain't right, Stevie thought. The others could have at least smiled at his jokes if they didn't want to laugh.

Stevie talked less and kept his eyes open.

Bo had already flipped that switch.

Suddenly, a metallic object glistened in the hot, dry afternoon sun. A tall lean dude, wearing a badly weathered process hairdo, brandished a firearm at his side. The gun, pointed downward, pressed against the thigh of a pair of baggy, worked-in Levi denims.

Stevie hoped Bo saw the gun, too, because he felt something was going to happen.

When the pack of young men had snailed its way to the corner of 59th Place, Stevie and Bo peeled off to cross the street to go home.

"Take it easy," Stevie said with an eerie reticence.

"Easy, Brian," said Bo.

"Later," Brian said as he and his clique kept strolling northward toward the railroad tracks.

Feigning calmness, Stevie and Bo waited for a space between the rush-hour caravan so they could cross Central Avenue and make it home. To take his mind off a bad feeling he had inside—the gang bangers, the old processed hairdo, the .38 caliber pistol—Stevie began playing Name That Car. "'59 Chevy Impala. '56 Pontiac. Sleek, candy-apple red '58 Ford Thunder Bird, convertible. '51 Chevy. '60 Chevy Corvair. '59 Coupe de Ville."

"'47 Studebaker," Bo chimed in.

Brian and his clique had walked a half block closer to the tracks. Maybe whatever was going to happen would happen on the other side of the tracks.

"'58 Chevy Impala—one of my favorites," Stevie said.

"'56 Pontiac," Bo blurted.

"'59 Chevy Corvette Stingray," shouted Stevie. "Lowriding Johnny Lopez's '51 Chevy with purple sponge dice bobbing on the rear-view mirror."

"Hey, there goes Calvin Simmons," Bo said pointing toward an off-colored black four-door '54 Buick going north.

Suddenly, the '54 Buick abruptly yanked over to the curve, screeched to a halt, cutting off Brian and his gang. Gregarious Nat Owens, a standout member of the Village Players, jumped out of the car before it stopped and socked one of

Brian's friends in the jaw. Sonny Boy jumped out of another door. Day-Day, one of the infamous Country Brothers, sprang from another.

Before Stevie and Bo could figure out what the Players were up to, a shot rang out, followed by another. The act was in place. Girls screamed and little boys walking home from school spinning their yo-yos ducked for cover.

But there were no utterances from the melee's principal players. The shooter possessed the spirit of the moment. Instead of fleeing north across the tracks, he ran back the opposite direction, south, to pursue his would-be assailants.

Stevie darted into the street and was almost hit by a screeching, honking rush-hour car. Feeling the shooter close distance quickly, Stevie instinctively ran in the opposite direction, away from home. Nat Owens ran low, west on 58th Drive. Sonny Boy and Day-Day ran low on the opposite side of the street using the honking cars as shields. Long, tall Calvin, still behind the wheel of his '54 Hog, ducked, held his brimmed hat on his head with one hand, stepped on the gas, and blindly rounded the corner, crashing into several moving and parked cars along the way.

Bo didn't run. He stood on the corner — straight up.

Bullets whistled — through trees. Wheee. Stevie's heart leapt from the thought that each bullet had his name on it. Perhaps the gunman felt that he, Stevie Roe, was on the front end of a conspiracy. Perhaps each runner felt the

same. The spirit of the moment was om-
nipresent.

Stevie cut south, hurdled one picket fence
and then another, running pass Sonny Boy's
house. He didn't have time to tell Sonny's
quizzical mother, standing on her front porch,
apron on, hands on hips, what all the ruckus
was about. Stevie ran fast, wondering for a moment how Bo made out.

*   *   *   *   *

"Dr. Stevie Roe, ain't seen you in five, ten
years it's been. Look the same. Ain't changed a
bit. How you been?"

Toothlessness, too much booze, and that old
throat wound warbled Bo's voice. Stevie strug-
gled to decipher what Bo was saying. But words
played a small role in how these two communi-
cated. Communication came equally through
body language, looks, and vocal intonation.
They both were saying without really saying it,
"I wish I could see you more often; life's a bitch."

"Fine," Stevie said. "And you?"

"Same old, same old…. How's your family?"

"Fine."

"What about your son? He must be in high
school by now? He into sports?"

"My son thinks he's tough. Growing freak-
ishly quickly. Seems he was just at my waist
the other day. Now he's threatening to look me
straight in the eyes.

"He's testing me at every inch of growth.
One inch, he wants to wrestle. Another inch, he
wants to box. As time moves on, he's winding up

in strength, and I'm trying to hold steady.

"He runs the hurdles, too. Perhaps he runs because I talk to him more about the way you and I used to run than I do about my profession.

"He understands instinctively what I mean when I say that the best defense is not a good offense. Left jabs, right crosses, and uppercuts make sense only under the Marquis of Queensbury's rules.

"War zones are unpredictable and, at best, have rules that are all too easily broken without consequence. In a war zone, guns and knives do not provide the best defense. They beget more of the same. In a war zone, the best defense is speed.

"Yes, speed. Not 'float like a butterfly, sting like a bee,' but dance dazzlingly unpredictably like the dragonfly. Dash with heart and loin; dart decisively and thoughtfully out of harm's way. Seize the air, then ride it.

"The same with life," Stevie said. "You've got to seize the air and then ride it."

Bo nodded reflectively, wondering why Stevie was so philosophical, so tense, so abstract.

Just as the last time they saw each other, their chance meeting peaked with the rerunning of that 100-yard dash. In Stevie's mind, that was the last great race.

When there was nothing more to share, Bo and Stevie stood quietly looking about each other. Bo looked terrible, wasted...all shot up and ragged. Stevie found it difficult to imagine this was the same kid with whom he had hawked the Sunday *Herald,* hustled bottles and unkempt lawns, and split nickel Butter Finger and Butter Nut candy bars; the boy who dusted Central Junior High's fastest runners thirty years ago with an awkward grace sketched indelibly in the memories of those who attended that track meet. And when the bullets flew, Bo had elected to stand his ground on the corner and, with the ultimate in courage or foolhardiness, peer into the approaching gunman's eyes.

"Life's a bitch," Bo mumbled, staring away blankly and shuffling an imaginary deck of cards. "Everybody gets a totally different hand dealt to them. A totally different hand."

Feeling guilt, then anger for feeling guilt, Dr. Roe's feelings began forming in his eyes. As the tears clouded his vision, he uttered in a whispered tenseness, "Why didn't you run low, Bo? Like the rest of us. Low! Hunh?"

Bo, still shuffling cards, peered with a tinge of melancholy and regret into his old friend's watery eyes. "Life ain't about living, but winning," he said. Then he paused and stared solemnly into the palm of his hands. "I did what I had to do, not what I should have done. I was a racer...not a runner."

Betrayed by his emotions, Dr. Stevie Roe abruptly turned his back to Bo Williams, walked briskly away from the corner, escaped into his air-conditioned mint green Jaguar sedan, scrubbed his thoughts with stereophonic jazz music, then inadvertently skidded onto Central Avenue away from the residual aftermath of his youth.

Bo remained standing on the corner flipping

cards and staring into his hands just the way Stevie had found him — sorrowful tobacco-colored eyes; a pitifully gaunt physique swallowed up by old, disheveled clothing; a mouth uttering sounds that children mocked then shortly disregarded. Again, Bo Williams stood alone...on the same corner he had stood on that momentous day thirty years ago...waiting for the Chevies, Fords, Pontiacs, and Buicks to go by. The price for standing tall? Martyrdom. A martyrdom that Bo could have appreciated only before he became one.

Randy Ross

Bitter

Dog

Randy Ross

typical Easter Sunday — damp and dull. Al's Wine and Beer, whose pattern of occupancy reflects the transience of the neighborhood, is probably the only thing open today. Even Al's, passersby might not recognize its line of business—the most prominent bit of I.D. being a paled Coca-Cola sign that's at least four proprietors old. Diehards, cement asses are rarities around these parts.

Many of the neighborhood "cats" who "copped" jobs after leaving Fremont High (the Pathfinder) — those with diplomas and luck — moved west, when possible, to Crenshaw, Adams, La Brea, to the "Jungle." They come "home" only on Halloween to help set the bonfire and to see what young buck will be the first to slither to the top of the grease pole. The rest of us remain steadfastly amidst our banal environs: either stuck but actively seeking an escape hatch, or despondently stuck and fed up with the American Dream.

Me and Lil Carl were hangin' out under Village Park's hacienda-like hooded porch on whose red brick surface folks play shuffleboard day-in-day-out during operating hours. There wasn't much to do. Same-old-same-old: cigarettes, Rainier Ale, Royal Crown Cola, pitching pebbles into nearby rain puddles, talking trash. Carl rapped about the scarcity of good weed and suggested we step back across the street to Al's to cop another brew. I wondered why the Park's restrooms were closed on holidays.

Later, ol' Jake eased coolly around the

building into view. Lil Carl, five-feet-six-and-a-half, wearing a "bad" tweed sports jacket, cuffed dacron polyester slacks, sporting a splendidly wrinkled pair of old folks comforts, stood, brim tilted, with his back against the dull, mud-colored wall. Slue-footed he stood, anticipating Jake's approach with a feigned passivity.

Jake, sauntering toward us with a glad-I-caught-up-with-you-brothers swagger, moved into the neighborhood about five years ago. We all went to junior high school together. Back then, he was as square as a pair of dice. Like a lost country boy landed in the city: tall, dark, skinny, timid, and hungry-looking. With time he had caught on to Los Angeles slumming—its subtleties, its fads. His dacrons were ostensibly aged and too high even for a flood, but Jake was cool—especially his heron-bone overcoat which he copped from the Salvation Army. That was the "thing" a year ago.

"Hey, what's goin' on, brothers," Jake said, slapping palms. "Get me high."

"What it is, brother," breezed Lil Carl. "You got it...."

I loathe that word "brother," particularly its utterance. I can write it all night long, but say it? Never. After the riots in '65, the term became sort of faddish. "Brother" this, or "sister" that. I guess it's okay, but I can't pipe it out of my throat right. "Brother," said correctly, that is using the Queen's English, is just too formal or too square. You might get chased down the street if you came off and said: "What's going on, bro-therz." Lil Carl would sometimes iterate that phrase in a mocking kind of way when he got high. If you played the line just right, like Carl, you might get a few good laughs. "Bro-therz." A good high was a must for all that primness.

On the other hand, I'm not going to adopt the illiterate form of the word: "brah-tha." It sounds stupid. I mean, I sound stupid saying it. But "brah-tha" is a prevalent, acceptable variant of "brother" in the ghetto. And everyone, including Jake, strokes it mellifluously—that is, all except me.

After '65, I still hung on stubbornly to phrases such as "What's happening?" or "Say, man?" or "Hey, baby" (you've got to be careful with that one) — which all, today, sound equally antiquated. But so does the typical mainstream line, "How are you?"

Later, big bad TG, an alumnus of the War Lords, ran across the street to the park and greeted us heartily.

"What you young bloods doing over here smack in the crack of Easter?"

Now that's some of that deep, inside talk; apparently Neanderthalish, but not necessarily so. Sub-cultural, subterranean bop.

And Jake laughed, too.

I took a stab at it, but it just wouldn't blow. It merely hissed — as if I wanted someone to smell my breath (which is only an "as if" because, in my opinion, bad breath is one hang-up the whole world suffers).

Carl started shadow boxing, shoe shuffling. "Man, what is you talkin' 'bout, ha, ha, ha?"

"Lil Carl, what is you doing?" TG said, tightening the crumpled paper sack at the nozzle of his bottle — undoubtedly a fifth of Bitter Dog — "chasing a ghost?"

Carl kept laughing, sparring, jiving. "You must be going downtown today," TG said. "All that pavement-scratching and tallyhooin', you go'n give them old folks comforts a heart attack."

Me and Jake fittingly chuckled. Egged TG right on. Carl kept on laughing and shadow boxing like he wanted go-some-chest with TG. I hoped Carl knew where to draw the line.

"And I'll tell ya," TG said, "I don't like to see nobody mess up a good pair of kicks; and, homeboy, if you don't freeze up on that slippin' and slidin', um go'n knock the Bo out o' yo' Jangles."

"HA, HA, HA," in unison, on time, and Carl stopped sparring, giving his soles a rest.

TG was in the pen for almost ten years. They say he used to press over 400 off the bench. When he came home in '63, he was twice as buffed as Steve Reeves. I remember his first day home he ran across the street from his mother's house, leaped over the Park rail, flung his shirt in the bushes, and brandished his upper torso. Awe-struck me. He was really mint—physically and mentally.

But that was seven years ago. Seven years without a lube job, the body and the mind squeak up on you like a rusty hinge. Wine, dope, and unemployment squeak up the works more. And for the greater portion of seven years, TG's been wine, dope, and no job. He said he learned to be a baker in the pen. Did have a job until his boss found out about his record. It's a wonder he never went back "up." But when you think about it, he's not the killer type, like Cornpuff or Jay-Jay Porter. He's more of a local county jail type than he is a San Quentin type, though he's been in Quentin.

"Yeah, God's done damn near gave everybody they share; pretty soon he should be struttin' through here to give me mine," TG said. "But, God, don't be too long in comin', I can't wait much longer. The man won't give me no job. The women won't act right; um broke; too old to be stayin' with my mama.... Naw, Lord, I can't wait too much longer. It's time to rain it on me. Mother may I take five iddy-biddy steps...?"

A while later, a fortyish little man sauntered around the building, fast like a Leprechaun.

"What's goin' on old dude?" TG said.

"How are ya, fellas?"

"Oh, I guess I'll make it," TG said, taking the lead.

Me, Jake, and Carl remained quiet but curious.

"Nice day," the man said.

"You got to be jivin'," TG staccatoed. "You hear that y'all, a nice day. Man, you got to be crazy, ha, ha, ha."

"No, really, when the rain dissipated, you know, and the sun shined through, it was nice, you know what I mean? A bit brisk perhaps.... You fellas mind sharing a bit of that jug?"

"This is my wine," TG said, holding up the

bottle possessively, as if he had been offended.

"Well, how about it fella?" the man said, his eyes alternating between the wine bottle and TG's eyes.

Having established ownership, TG relented. "Yeah, it's Easter, you can have a swig, home-boy."

TG handed over the sack-covered fifth of Bitter Dog, and the man turned it up, gulped greedily but briefly, then brought it back down.

"Aah," he sighed, passing the bottle back. "Well, I've gotta get going. I'll see you fellas around." He then walked quickly across the baseball field toward Naomi Way.

Ceremoniously, TG wiped the nozzle of his bottle briskly with his shirt tail; then, sticking his baby finger inside the bottleneck, he whirled it like an agitator. Finally, he lifted the bottle from the brown paper sack and held it up for inspection.

"Ain't that a bitch!" TG said. "Homeboy damn near downed all my grape. I'll be a dirty whore's pimp."

Me and Carl laughed demonstrably.

"You know, something told me not to give that sucker no wine. I told him to take a swig, and look what he did. I might as well go ahead and kill this."

TG turned the bottle up until its contents emptied, caught the final drops with his outstretched tongue, then threw the bottle up and out beyond the porch. The bottle hit the pavement, bursting clamorously, perhaps the zillionth christening of that sidewalk area.

"Give a man a inch, he snatch a whole yard," TG said. "That's what the man has been doing to us for 400 years. We built this country. We're responsible for the deliverance of this hemisphere. It was sweat and blood off the backs of our forefathers. Then they promised us forty acres and a mule, and what we get? Who you know got forty acres today? You know anybody got forty acres?"

"Naw, man," I said.

"What about y'all? Jake? Lil Carl?"

"Naw," they said shaking their heads in the negative, with a tinge of embarrassment as if they were unforgivably ignorant of something critically important to their lives.

Personally, I don't have a strong attachment to land or property. I mean, you live in a house, you have a place to sleep, food to eat, an indoor toilet, a hi-fi set, a black and white television that doesn't blink a lot, and your folks pay the rent. Sometimes they move, maybe down the street, even when you don't want them to move. But it's not a real big deal. That's the way things are. Bags is the only one I know whose parents own land and property. So what? Me, Lil Carl, Jake. We're all in the same boat. Even TG. But for some reason, this land question gnaws at him incessantly.

"Cause it ain't nobody," TG said. "You know damn well that if the Indian could be tricked out of a whole continent, forty acres could be taken from one of us—real easy. My grandfather's one of the few cats around here who owns anything this side of one acre, that ant hill you see over 'cross the street. And now, here it is Easter Sunday, and the trickin' goes on like a runaway train."

TG looked toward Naomi Way, in the direction the man was walking. Me and Lil Carl fought off hysterical laughter. "Easter Sunday. This is the day the Lord.... You know, I ought not let that sucker get away with that.

"Damn right," resolved TG as he began trotting toward the man.

"Hey, brother?" shouted TG, flanking his mouth with both hands.

The man turned around and looked.

"Hold it down for a second."

The man paused and the distance between him and TG converged. Finally, they were face-to-face, TG faintly panting from the trot (that's his history). They started talking and gesturing. I couldn't hear them well, but the conversation went something like this:

"What is it?" the man said.

"Can you put a quarter on another bottle of Bitter Dog?"

"Wish I could, fella, but um plum broke," replied the man, patting his pockets for proof.

"You mean to tell me you ain't got a dime?"

"Not a thing. Really. If I had it, I'd give it to ya. You know what I mean?"

"Yeah, un hunh, I know exactly what you mean," muttered TG, clenching his teeth.

"Sorry, brother."

"Brother, my ass," TG said tensely, attempting to hit the man with a lurching 180 degree roundhouse punch.

The man ducked under the heavy, revolving fist, then darted backward about two feet and wrought a tentative martial arts stance.

Disgruntled and unmoved by the stance, TG stepped forward, circled back with a left hook, missed again and this time slipped to the ground, gasping for air, spent.

Then the man said somewhat timorously, "Fella, why you wanna do that? I didn't do anything to ya."

Inspecting the grass stains on his jacket, TG looked up at the man angrily and dumbfoundedly, panted, spat, and stared. But he didn't say a word.

The man, sensing the apparent ineptness of his would-be assailant, cautiously backed away several yards, turned and walked away hastily.

We stood on the porch perplexed by the spectacle. I wanted to laugh out so bad, but I knew I should check myself. TG was seething.

As the man faded in the distance, TG, in a rather odd fashion, let the force of gravity lull his body into a prone position—undoubtedly a move to salvage his "cool." He knew he had just blown a trillion points, now he had to try to get some back. It didn't take him long to realize that one simply does not flop down on the grass after it rains. Once that water seeped trough his clothing, he jumped up in a flash, flinching from the chill of the water. So he lost more points.

Damn, did I want to laugh. Lil Carl, facing Al's, his back to TG, couldn't hold it.

Jake was cool. He never does laugh out. Ever since he came to Los Angeles, he's been timid. Even now, he just laughed sort of gently — in, not out.

And so, this time, listening to Carl's laughter, and thinking that Jake must be quite slow to laugh so gently, my tickle box exploded. I laughed so hard I had to clutch my stomach. This only transported Carl to hysterical laughter. For a while, our bodies jerked spasmodically. Jake kept cool.

It seemed a long time before TG made it back to the shelter of the roofed porch. When he did, oddly enough he was smiling. By then, we had about petered out of laughter.

Though still watery-eyed and my nose yet sniffling, I managed to pop the clean-up question, "What happened?", very seriously, mind you.

"I slipped," TG said, wiping futilely at a grass stain on his pants.

He had to do better than that. We all knew he slipped, or plunged, after the second swing. So when he said he slipped, we stood silently restraining our guts, and awaited...something.

"It's the same old game," TG said. "It's like the Emancipation Proclamation and Reconstruction. It's like getting an education and Urban Renewal. The man just keep on tellin' us that if we try hard to pick ourselves up by the bootstraps, you dig, then we can catch up with mainstream America. But soon as we almost there, he know we out of gas. He knows this. So we fall back down again. We end up goin' through the same old jive all over again. That's why the Civil Rights Movement ain't.... Say, looka here, Jake, you got half on a bottle of Bitter Dog?"

Randy Ross

Fathers

and

Sons

Randy Ross

y father regrets my future because in it he sees the end of his own.

"Son, you've got to stop going around getting drunk and acting a fool."

"Drunk? Daddy, I'm not the only one around here who drinks."

"Junior, what I do is not your concern. What you ought to be doing is figuring out how to take care of your children and get them and their mother off the county."

"So when did you become a big-time champion of the family? From what I remember, you weren't one before. 'Cause if you were, Mama wouldn't be out there living by herself in some dinky little apartment."

"Junior, what's the matter with you? Every time I try to tell you something, you run off and tug on your mama's dress. Instead of worrying about everybody else's business, you need to get your own act together. Find a job so you can feed your family and make sure they got more than a leaky roof over their heads. It's your responsibility—not mine—to make sure my grandkids ain't go'n be goin' to school with holes in their socks."

I threw my hands into the air. "I give up! You got me. Now since you have all the answers, why don't you tell me where I can get a decent job."

"Go out there and find one. If I did it with a fifth grade education, you damn sure ought to be able to do it."

"Daddy, do you..."

"Junior," he interjected before I could finish my thought, "I don't want to hear that nonsense about you can't find no job. Your problem is you're lazy. When you and your sister were but so high, I wore out many a pair of shoes hunting down work. So don't tell me you can't find no job. Go tell that to somebody else."

"That's what I'll do," I shouted.

Before my father could slash me with another word, I stormed out of his house.

I made it back to the house the next morning. It was still dark outside. My father was waiting up for me. He was half drunk and so was I. I turned on the television, flipped the channel to an old black-and-white western movie, then flopped down on the plastic-covered loveseat. The wooden floor creaked as he stumbled to the television and clicked it off. He had to be real pissed off because he's nuts about westerns.

The man, my father, stood between me and his television looking like a charcoal statue of a stocky blue collar worker. He gazed down on me with fire-filled eyes.

"Why you do that?" I said.

His gaze sharpened. Then his mouth spun that same old scratched record.

"Junior, you look for work today?"

"What you think?"

"I don't think anything; I know you didn't."

"That's the problem. You know everything, and I don't know shit."

My father poked himself hard in the chest. "Boy, this is my house. You don't use that kind of language 'round here. Not in my house!"

I had intended to apologize, but I ended up saying something else.

"Yeah, but this ain't my mother's house."

"Junior, your problem is that you got your head stuck up so far into everybody else's past that your future looks like shit."

The next thing I knew, I had jumped up in his face and started shouting. "I'm a man, goddamn it!"

He rushed me swinging his fists. I grabbed him and we wrestled around the living room like bears until we crashed into the television. In shock, he ran his fingers along the crack in the glass screen. Meanwhile I quietly stuffed my large nylon duffle bag and eased through the front door. I shouldn't have been fighting my father, but he kept messing with me. The last thing I remember, the old man was perched on the porch shouting he was going to blow my brains out. As soon as I heard his shotgun click, I put my head down and ran like a buffalo in a stampede.

* * * * *

Dazed, I strolled the streets thinking about my father, mother, kids. Somehow I wound up at Bethune Park, where acres of memories lay buried in the damp ground. Here, as a kid I had played little league baseball and football. During my high school days, I had shot hoops every day. Lately I have been hanging out with some of the guys I grew up with, played ball with, fought with, chased girls with, ditched school with, got high with. But I try not to hang out anyplace too long. And it's easy to tell when you've been around a place too long—you have run out of good stories to tell, and nobody has any to tell you. But I felt easy here.

I pulled my old blanket from my duffle bag and snuggled under a table in the wooded picnic area. But I couldn't rest. I kept thinking and squirming and listening to the wind.

Around four that morning, I got up, stuffed my blanket into my duffle bag, and began making my way toward Central Avenue. Through a tall chainlink fence, vicious junk-yard dogs growled at a stray mutt. Other than that, the sidewalks were empty. The morning night was so people-quiet that I imagined I owned the city streets and the high arching street lights that peered through the fog.

A few miles down, I spotted an empty all-night donut shop. I bought a large cup of coffee, plopped down at a choice table by a window that gave the widest view of Central Avenue, lit a cigarette, then stirred lots of sugar and cream into the steaming black liquid. Cars passed occasionally; I counted them and tried to see if I knew their drivers. Between cars, I scratched at my predicament by humming tunes and messaging my foam cup as hard as I could without crushing it.

Before daybreak, dull-eyed workers began piling into the coffee shop with "another day" scowls etched in their faces. I bought fresh glaze donuts, waved at the baker as I exited the shop, then made my way toward the old shack on the corner of 59th and Hooper.

The men who hang out at the shack — men like Mr. Macon, Mr. Garvey, Old Man Slim, and Sweet Buddy Dee — are the men who built it. Not so long ago, nothing graced that lot but a bunch of trash. Then we came in, took over, and built a makeshift shelter. We made the walls out of a bunch of old boards and what was left of a white picket fence that had been dumped in the lot. We furnished the shack with milk crates, a smoked-out sofa from a house that burned up across the street, and a faded green Naugahyde recliner that Mr. Garvey donated. It rained hard one day, so we put up a roof using a few boards, strips of tin, and old plastic drop cloths. Then we got this big steel barrel for a fireplace when it gets cold at night.

When I made it to the corner, none of the regulars had showed up yet. I stepped into the shack and flopped down in the Naugahyde recliner, taking care not to sit on a coiled spring poking up through the middle like a headless jack-in-the-box. It didn't feel right being around the shack so early in the morning, especially since no one else was around. But I couldn't think of a better place to go.

Later Sweet Buddy Dee cruised into the lot in his old mauve Cadillac. The way he tells it, in his heyday he was a super pimp and a hell of a gambler. He swears he hasn't hit fifty yet, but it looks like life has beat a lot more years than that out of him. He still wears conk in his head because he says "most people in the world can't stand nappy hair around 'em, and pimpin's a people business." He still prefers iridescent slacks because "so much color in 'em, the ladies think I'm complex and exciting." He hardly ever takes off his felt Stetson hat because he says he's always on the move. He still wears pointed-toed Stacy Adams shoes, which he says are real good for "kickin' ho's and joes." And gold-filled cavities weigh down the front of his mouth, which he figures shows he's been successful.

The passenger door of Sweet Buddy Dee's car opened and Old Man Slim stepped out. He had to be the oldest of the regulars. But I don't know how old he is, what he did for a living, who his family is, or nothing. All I know is he has a mean streak in him. Always fucking with somebody.

"Boy, I heard you was sleepin' in the park last night," Slim shouted as he limped toward the shack. "What's the matter? You ain't got a place to stay?"

"Sure I have a place to stay," I shouted back. "Who told you I was sleeping in the park last night? You think I'm a bum or something?"

I was angry with myself for raising my voice. I reached into my duffle bag for the donuts I bought earlier that morning.

"Y'all have some?"

Sweet Buddy Dee rubbed his stomach. "No thank you, Junior. Them ham, eggs, and grits my woman fixed me this mo'nin' are still talkin' to each other."

"Man, ain't no woman fixed you breakfast,"

Old Man Slim hissed. "You ate at Norm's Restaurant this morning just like I did."

Everybody laughed.

Sweet Buddy Dee regrouped. "But didn't you see the waitress who served me? Well, she was my woman."

Old Man Slim laughed up a storm. "Yeah, and I s'pose that humpty-dumpty fellow in the kitchen who cooked your food was your man."

I laughed out loud and so did Sweet Buddy Dee.

Later, Mr. Macon and Mr. Garvey came by the shack. Mr. Macon worked on a good-paying government job before retiring and pulling a nice, steady pension. His youngest son, Bobby, and I went to grade school together.

Mr. Garvey slaved for about fifty years as a brick mason and carpenter before he quit working. He knows my father real well from hooking him up with a few construction jobs.

I wondered if Mr. Garvey knew about what happened last night. But he didn't mention anything close to it until later that night after everybody had left the shack except the two of us.

"Everything all right, Junior?"

"Sure," I said.

Mr. Garvey then went on home. I slouched down in the Naugahyde chair wide awake and followed each of his footsteps. After I lost sight of him, I reached into my wallet for a small photograph of my little girl and boy kneeling at a Christmas tree excitedly ripping gift wrap from boxes of toys I had carted into the house.

Later that night, my older sister, Debra,

drove up to the shack in her little Ford Escort and told me that Mama said I could stay at her place until I got a job.

"Sis, how did you know to find me here?"

"You ain't a hard man to find, Junior. You leave tracks everywhere."

I felt small knocking on my mother's front door. If Debra had not been looking from her car, I would have left before Mama answered.

Mama opened the door and said, "Come on in, Junior," and I walked into her apartment.

Debra honked her horn, waved, and drove off.

"Debra said she'll be by this weekend," I said.

"That child always comes by to see about me."

I knew what Mama was aiming at, so I didn't give her a target. Instead, I kept quiet and looked around her stuffed little apartment. Pictures of my sister and me were everywhere. Spring was almost over, but Christmas cards still decorated the portal leading to the bedroom. Just beneath the gold-framed photo of John-Martin-Robert, my little league basketball and baseball trophies crowded the top of the oval-faced floor-model television that my father had picked up at a government auction years ago. Probably, he had let Mama have that television only because it was on the blink. But it didn't matter to Mama that the television didn't work.

I put down my duffle bag by the front door

and sat down in a frayed, rusty-legged chair at the old metal dinette that had been around since I was a kid — another of the few things Mama had managed to tow with her when she and Daddy split.

Without my asking, Mama heated me a big bowl of leftover neckbone stew. After downing the stew, I dozed off at the table.

"Junior! Child, I don't mind so much you sleeping at the table, but before you do, take this towel and washcloth and go bathe yourself."

Everything started off fine at Mama's. But after a couple of days, she started telling me the same old stuff my father had been rubbing in. But she did it with a high-pitched honeydew voice.

"Junior, when are you going to bring my grandbabies by here to see me? When was the last time you saw your children? You know those kids need their father. Junior, you been looking for work?"

What do they know about the way things are today? They didn't have to go through what I'm going through. I have looked and looked. I have nearly starved standing in lines that wrapped around downtown corners just to get a job application. Then when I do get a job, they wonder why I don't hold on to it. They don't know what it feels like to have a year of college and then to have to scrounge for work that pays peanuts and uses less than half of what I know. Everybody from their generation bowed down, so they figure I got to bow down, too. But to hell with that!

Junior this; Junior that. Just more put-downs. And a put-down is a put-down, no matter how sweet the voice. So not long after I started staying at Mama's, I messed around and got drunk, went home to her place, and started bad-talking her. It was pitiful the way she cried and shouted that no child of hers would talk to her that way.

"Mama, I'm a man. I am twenty-three years old and I need to be respected like a man and not treated like some snotty nose, nappy head boy."

She stopped talking, locked herself in the bathroom, and kept crying up a storm. She never did tell me I had to go, but I knew it was time. The way I look at it, there ain't much worse in life than a man staying around his mother so long she has to tell him to go. It's best to leave before that, even if you slide down to skid row. At least, that way, you could feel that if things ever got too bad in the streets, you had a place you could go to rest your head.

* * * * *

Since falling out with Mama, I've been coming to the shack every day. When the old men see me hanging around in the morning, they hassle me about not working or looking for a job, and back it up with talk about Great Depression times when a colored man would work all day for less than a dollar. But when the old men put me down, it doesn't tick me off as much as when my folks do it. And they all say pretty much the same stuff. But the way the old men at the shack criticize you, it's sort of a ritual...like they're holding the gate open for those of us who haven't gone through yet. And the old men lay it on heavy. But I take it in stride, hardly mustering up any arguments to try to explain my predicament. It doesn't rub me the wrong way because they talk to me like I'm a man.

"Jobs are out there," Mr. Garvey lectured, "but young Negroes today won't work 'cause they say the wages is low. I say you've got to start somewhere! Why if I would have had the educational and job opportunities you young men have today, I woulda been a hell of a man. Hell of a man!"

"Who ever told y'all that it was about work?" Sweet Buddy Dee chimed in. "That's a myth. It's all about money. And whoever said you had to work to get money? That's another myth. I am living proof of that, baby."

"I will never lay another brick or hammer another nail in my life if I don't want to," Mr. Garvey stated matter-of-factly. "My slaving days are over. All I got to do from now on is rest, dress, and read the *Free Press*."

Then Old Man Slim had to agitate. "Man, you don't know what in the hell you talkin' 'bout. You can't read!"

"Fuck you Slim." Mr. Garvey must have been real pissed off, because he hardly ever uses profanity.

"I can't read worth a damn either," Sweet Buddy Dee jumped in, "but with that big El Dorado, these fine threads, and all this gold in my mouth, I bet y'all think I can read faster than Bob Hayes could run the hundred."

Then I added my two cents to the conversation. "Now if readin' is the issue, y'all need to be talkin' about Mr. Macon's son, Bobby. Bobby Macon can read fly shit. I know. I went to school with him. Teacher tell the class to read a story, and she catch Bobby sleeping at his desk and hit him with a ruler and say, 'Young Man, you're supposed to be reading the story, not dreaming. Read the story or I'll send you to the Principal's Office.' And what you think Bobby did? Bobby said, 'Why did you hit me, Mrs. Copling, I finished reading the story.' Then Mrs. Copling tried to set a trap for him. She said, 'Oh, you have, have you? Well, Bobby Macon, stand up and tell the class what the story was about.' I held my breath, because I just knew Mrs. Copling had Bobby by the balls. Everybody, including me, thought Bobby was go'n look the fool. But Bobby told that story so good that I didn't have to finish readin' it. Mrs. Copling hated that he told that story so good. All she could think to do was cut him off before he finished and tell him to sit down and keep his eyes open. I'll tell you, Bobby Macon can read his ass off. Tell 'em Mr. Macon."

"Yeah, the boy is pretty good with the books," Mr. Macon reflected. "These days ain't like the old days. Today you got to have some education. Take Bobby, for instance. He been goin' to school all his life. He done graduated from high school, done graduated from college, and now he still goin' to school in New York City to get a master's degree. See, that boy got education smokin' out his ears. Now I'm not saying y'all need all that education, but you need at least to have a high school diploma in your hands when you go 'round looking for a job that's going to pay any kind of decent money. These days, a pimp will be a broke ass pimp if he ain't got some education. That's all there is to it."

Then Old Man Slim, with his narrow ass, said, "Yeah, Brother Macon, that boy of yours got so much education, you must feel like a dinosaur around him."

"Naw. It don't work that way. You see, he may have book knowing, but I've got mother wit. Sure, I ain't got much schooling. But for them times, I got a pretty good education. I read and write and compute with the best of 'em. Besides all that, I don't care how much education he gets, he is still my son. I brought him into this world and raised him up to be where he is today. Understand what I mean?"

Early that evening, Bobby came down to the corner looking for Mr. Macon.

"Daddy, Mama said to come eat supper."

Bobby saw me under the shack cooling it and we shook hands and talked a little while. I asked him how the New York City chicks were treating him.

"Fine," he said. "Just fine. Brother, whatever you do in life, you must visit the Big Apple at least once."

"Maybe I can go back with you so I can get the hell out of this hole."

Laughing, Bobby asked me how I was doing. "Fine," I lied. Had I told him the truth, he would have wanted to know why. It wasn't worth the trouble.

Just as Bobby was getting around to asking me about my family, Mr. Macon caught his attention.

"Bobby, go to the sto' and get me and Old Man Slim, here, a Budweiser."

As Bobby eased around the corner to the store, Mr. Macon blew his nose, put his handkerchief back in his pocket, and held his head high while spying Old Man Slim's expression.

"Like I say Slim, I don't care how much education he got, he is still my boy."

Bobby came back from the store, pulled a can of soda out of the bag for himself and handed the rest to his father. Mr. Macon took the two cans of beer from the sack and handed one to Old Man Slim.

"What the hell you get me a short can of beer for?" Slim complained. "I only drink tall ones."

"I'm sorry, sir, but I didn't know what size to get, so I got regular."

"Shit, you ought to know to get a tall can. You s'posed to have education enough to know better. What in the world they teachin' y'all in them colleges and universities anyway? I ain't go'n drink this skimpy can of beer."

Mr. Macon broke in. "Bobby, take this dollar and go get Mr. Slim a tall can of beer."

"I'm not going to get it," snapped Bobby. "If he wants a tall can of beer, someone else will have to get it for him, 'cause I ain't go'n hit a lick at a snake."

Old Man Slim had to agitate. "Boy, yo'

daddy told you to go get me a tall can of beer, didn't he? So, damn it, go on get me that beer like you got some sense!"

Bobby Macon paused and looked Old Man Slim straight in the eyes. "Sir, if the beer were for my father, I'd gladly get it for him. But, with all due respect, you can kiss my black ass." Bobby then walked on home away from the shack.

Now that sounded more like the Bobby I used to know when we were coming up. He had me wondering about him with all that "Yes, Sir" shit.

With Bobby gone, Old Man Slim lit into Mr. Macon.

"Macon, yo' boy ain't shit."

But Mr. Macon pulled a reversal.

"If he woulda kissed your ass, Slim, he would not have been shit. He's *my* son, not yours. Old as you is, you should be wise enough in your ways to understand that."

"All Macon, you talkin' a bunch of bullshit."

"Well, Slim, like the boy said, kiss my ass and give me back my beer."

Mr. Macon snatched the unopened can of beer from Old Man Slim and handed it to me. I popped the top, took a swallow before Slim could say anything, and thanked Mr. Macon at the end of a burp. I felt Old Man Slim staring down on me with his tiny, wine-colored, spider-webbed eyes sunk in his drawn up, snag-a-tooth face.

"Don't mention it, son," Mr. Macon said as he went home for supper behind Bobby.

Old Man Slim started heeing and hawing about Mr. Macon and Bobby, how they were just a couple of Indian givers. I was feeling pretty good by this time, so I told him to shut up or get out of my shack.

Sweet Buddy Dee cut into me for laying claim. "How in the fuck this yo' shack?"

Old Man Slim had to get a piece of me, too. "That boy ought to be evicted for not payin' rent."

"Y'all leave Junior be," Mr. Garvey said. "He just come on hard times. He knows this here shack belongs to everybody."

It seems I should be able to do better, keep a steady job, own a home, and help my mother get out of that matchbox apartment. But nothing ever falls in place for me.

As far as my kids' mother is concerned; we're never going to get back together. No way. Every chance she gets, she tells me I ain't shit; I say she ain't shit either. If I don't keep away, I'll probably end up killing her...or she'll end up killing me. Either way, our kids might end up in the shit house, tossed from one relative to the next wondering if they would ever have a place they could call home. Worse than that, they might live the rest of their lives trying to understand or not think about why their mother and father messed over each other the way they did and never gave their children a chance to have a regular family.

I don't know. Some people think that everybody's fate is determined from the get-go. For all I know this patched-up shack may be my fate. So be it. Just give me my hand and I'll play the cards the way they're dealt. I'm a man, goddamn it! Just like all the other men who come around here.

Before Mr. Garvey left the shack that night, he looked straight at me like he was worried. He knew by now what had happened between me and my father. And he and the other men knew that I had slept outside at the park...more than once. But nobody talked about it. Not even Old Man Slim. But nobody could claim that I ever slept in the shack. Nobody!

"So, Mr. Garvey, when you reckon this old shack comin' down?"

"Junior, I don't really know. But nothing lasts forever. New things are always croppin' up to push out the old things. It ain't always to my liking, but I appreciate that the world is set up that way. Son, you just have to figure out a way to deal with it. 'Cause I'll tell you, Junior, we don't need no more cart pushers."

"Yes, sir."

After Mr. Garvey left that night, I didn't feel comfortable staying around the shack. I grabbed my duffle bag and started walking. I had no place to go; I just wanted to walk.

About ten o'clock that night, I stepped onto my father's creaky wooden porch as quietly as I could. I eased the duffle bag off my shoulder and rested it on an old rusty chair on the porch.

The television blared. Daddy must have gotten it fixed. I heard horses galloping, neighing. It was a western movie.

I stood at the door with my head bowed. I took deep breaths. I could smell damp porch wood, grass, and nearby wild flowers. Blood rushed through my head; I messaged my pulsating temples.

I raised my chin. I straightened my body. I knocked on my father's door.

He didn't answer, so I knocked again, harder this time.

"Who is it?" my father shouted.

"Me!" I said loud enough to be heard.

"The door's open," he said.

I lit a cigarette, took a long drag, and then flicked it out toward the street.

I heard my father laugh at the movie.

I picked up my duffle bag.

"Junior, the door is open," he repeated.

I went in and closed the door....

Gingerbread

Girl

Randy Ross

ell, officer, as I told you before, I met her in a storm in the middle of the week. Central Avenue. South. It was Tuesday, after midnight. Cold, windy, wet.

Done with finals, I needed to hang loose. The last exam had been a bear. Operations research. Explaining the mathematical connection between the simplex algorithm and duality theory had locked my jowls all day. So after work that night, I rushed to Easy Times Bar and Pool Hall to shake off stress.

Well, sir, to me Central Avenue is not as bad you think. I grew up in this neighborhood. I know the people and the places. On Central Avenue, people are real because they have to be. And on good nights the neon girls buzz and dance.

Good nights? Just tap beer, pistachios, fast talk, and a nail-biting game of nine-ball.

Girls? Not really. Few girls around Easy Times anymore except weary older ones scrubbing poverty and man problems with tap beer and loud blues music.

I waited for Coota, Slick, John B., Pee-Wee to ease through the door to run nine-ball for a buck a game. But hardly anybody showed up. I had to settle for bottled Schlitz and a slow game of eight-ball with old man Slim who, as usual, rambled nonstop.

No, sir, I don't know if Slim knew the girl. He was gone before she came. When Easy Times closed I had offered him a ride home. But he waved me off and wobbled down Central Avenue smiling as the rain beat a tune on his gray plastic raincoat and porkpie hat. After Slim became a soundless shadow in the night, I stepped next door to the Chicken Shack for something to soak up the brew in my belly.

The first time I saw the girl, it had to be after two in the morning. She peered through the slit in the window of the passenger door of my seven-year-old '63 Mercury-Monterey—portable haven for a po' boy. Trench coat drenched. Shoes in hand. Barefooted. Feet wet, hair wet, face wet. Mascara-smudged eyes.

"Baby, honey child, spin me out of the rain," she said.

"Where you headed?" I asked.

"Home," she said.

"Where is home?"

"Not far, honey. Please!"

"But I don't know you," I said.

"I'm a sister," she said, "and you're a brother. You warm up in your car and I get rained on. I am a sister. So, brother, you go'n let me stand here and catch something?"

"That depends on what you're fishing for," I said. "But while you're thinking about it, sit in my car out of the rain."

"Thank you, but I don't need to sit," she said. "I need to get home."

"But I don't know you," I said.

"Ain't I a sister? Are you a brother?"

"Yeah. Right. But sit down and dry up while I down this fried chicken."

"But, man, I must get home," she said.

I pushed the passenger door open and waved her in. She paused, eyed me suspiciously, irritated at my slowness in gravitating to her need. Chipped red fingernails, hands bent on tilted trench coat hips, she doll-eyed me and didn't blink. And then her head bowed and fresh tears leaked.

No, sir, I don't know why she cried. She looked sad, angry. No, I don't know why she was angry, but I was pissed off, too. And hungry. How can a po' boy enjoy fried chicken when a tall gingerbread girl stands barefooted in the rain staring at him with leaking hazel eyes?

"You hungry?" I said.

"Why are you so cold?" she said. "What did I do to make you treat me this way?"

"But I don't even know you!" I said.

"I trusted you," she said.

No, sir, I have no idea why she talked to me that way...as if she knew me long and deep.

So then I plopped my fried chicken snack on the passenger seat. "Sit down and eat," I said, "I'll go and get another one."

She didn't budge. Kept right on crying.

Yes, sir, I got her into my car. What else could I do? She was crying. I darted into the rain and gently guided her to the seat, got her out of the rain. Her porous shell chilled, too goosed to thaw.

After plucking my keys from the ignition, I sloshed down the rain-pecked sidewalk past Riker's barbershop, the vacant shoeshine parlor, the storefront holiness church, and Easy Times. I finally reached the Chicken Shack, its fogged windows striped with iron security bars.

Yes, sir, I left the girl in the car alone. No, I don't recall locking the doors.

When I stepped through the front door of the Chicken Shack, a loud buzzer sounded. The chef-hatted dark old man, Unc, sat calmly behind the counter poring over a *Jet* magazine.

"Hey, Unc," I said, "whip me up another chicken dinner to go."

Unc dressed half a nude chicken in thick batter then tonged it into a vat of sizzling dark oil. "A bird ain't got a chance in the world with you hungry young bucks on the prowl," he said.

"What bird?" I said.

"The one in the deep fry," Unc said. "Careful 'fore she burn you."

No, sir, I don't know if Unc saw or knew the girl. I thought he meant the chicken in the vat, not the girl in my car.

While waiting for the chicken, fries, roll, and sliced sweet pickles, I dropped a quarter in the jukebox and pressed J2 twice to hear Sonny Criss wail on "Sunrise, Sunset."

No, sir, I did not hear any gunshots outside.

When Unc handed me the bag of new hot chicken, I breezed back toward my car snapping my fingers in three-quarter time. I snapped past Easy Times, past the holiness church, past the shoeshine parlor.

But when I made it to Riker's barbershop, I froze. Something had gone wrong. The passenger window of my po' boy's haven had exploded into kaleidoscopic shards of green, purple, blue, red, pink.

I moved closer. Light flowed from the glove compartment. My eyes darted about Central Avenue searching for clues. Nothing.

I eased around to the driver side of the car and stepped close enough to press the door knob. When the door opened, there were soft, piercing squeaks I had not noticed before now. As I stood there stuck, my hands began to shake and the rain wet my velour bucket seats. Traces of perfume, charcoal, burnt sulfur punctured the air. The glove compartment had been ransacked and chicken was scattered everywhere.

That's when I saw the pistol with the pearl handle. Small, pretty. It glistened in the low light from the glove compartment.

No, sir, it's not my gun. Sure, I'm sure. No, I don't own a gun.

After leaning on the car to keep my balance I flopped down in the driver seat, squeezed the steering wheel, and peered straight down Central Avenue until the street lights converged to a point.

I thought about calling the police, but it didn't seem to matter.

I rested her head on my lap. She seemed smaller, thinner than when she first stood by the car.

No, sir, my pants didn't feel wet; I didn't feel any blood. I didn't feel anything. I just wanted to rock her to sleep.

Why? Well, it was because of the note she scribbled on a yellow paper napkin that had been used to wrap a broken wishbone. The napkin was wet and the ink smeared, but I could

make out the words: "Thanks for the ride. Love,
Sonora." The note was for me. Who else could
it have been for? I slashed through my head for
snatches of memory. Had I known her before, I
would know her now. Wouldn't I?

I got the blanket out of the trunk and covered her body. I started the car and turned on
the radio. I knew she loved Oldies But Goodies.
I just knew it. In the rain and quiet dark, I
drove slowly down Central Avenue toward that
point in the distance where the street lights
met.

No, sir, I wasn't trying to conceal her. I put
the blanket over her body because of the rain,
the wind, the cold.

At Imperial Highway, a traffic light brought
the po' boy's haven to a stop as The Robins
crooned their hit, "Since I First Met You." Then
a strong breeze swooped through the hole in the
passenger window and sucked out the song,
leaving only static on the radio. Suddenly the
girl felt as light as a hollow log. It no longer
mattered that her feet were bare, her make-up
smudged, her hair pasty wet, her nut-colored
eyes shut. She had flown home with a song. Her
song. Our song.

Postscript

hen I began subscribing to *Story* a few years back, I developed a habit of going to the back of the publication to pore over what the authors had to say about their stories. Some fiction writers cited origins that were clear and crisp; others' statements seemed vague or abstruse. Still other writers apparently cannot consciously uncover the source(s) of their creative journeys. The writers' reflections fascinated me and often caused me to view their corresponding stories in different, sometimes more personally rewarding, ways.

Readers, listeners have asked me — sometimes implicitly — how my stories come to life. Because the answer is almost always complex, I have tended to duck the question. *Story*, however, has led me to ascribe value to information on how writers come by their fictions. This book's introduction recounts the origin of the story, "The Chocolate Man." At the risk of revealing too much about myself, I will attempt in this postscript to say something about the origins, sources, or motivation behind the other stories in this book: "Red's Rhythm," "Grape Rain," "Conjure Women," "When Are They Coming," "Robbie the Genie," "Run Low," "Bitter Dog," "Fathers and Sons," and "Gingerbread Girl."

Red's Rhythm

About 3 am on a day in 1987, I was compelled to get out of bed and rush to my study, turn on my computer, and begin transcribing the words of a hip old man who had lived in New Orleans during the 1940s. The old man talked a lot about dancing and he constantly reminded me that his name was Red. He talked and I typed until daybreak.

"Red's Rhythm" was created from some of what Red told me. The story first appeared in the 1994 anthology, *River Crossings: Voices from the Diaspora*, published by International Black Writers and Artists (IBWA). "Red's Rhythm" has also received some attention as a performance piece; it was recognized by the HBO New Writers' project in late 1994.

I suspect Red will visit me again to recount more of his life's story. Maybe I'll have to take a trip to New Orleans to look him up.

Grape Rain

Beginning the late 1980s every morning I would drive the kids to Transfiguration, a parochial school in southwest Los Angeles. Over time the ride to school became a fun time for me and the kids. We played car games (most of which we created), the kids did their homework or, on Fridays, studied for their spelling test. And I learned to listen to rap music.

One morning we were exploring ideas for a story (one of the girls had an assignment to write a short story) and up jumped this idea of a boy who, while hanging out at the railroad tracks in the rain, sees grapes raining down from the sky.

The girls never used this idea. However a few years later I developed the story, "Grape

Rain," to illustrate the difficulty of separating reality from make-believe. It was published in *Maryland Review* (1993) — my first published story. The author's byline enabled me to acknowledge the contributions of my two youngest children, Carolyn and Lee-Madeline. They proudly took the journal to school to share the story with their teachers.

Conjure Women

When I returned to Los Angeles in the early 1980s to pursue a Ph.D., my young family and I moved into Antell Marshall's apartment building on East 41st Street, across the street from Ross Snyder Park (known for its baseball diamonds). Only elderly women lived there when we first arrived. We got to know them well. They were especially fond of our children — Dennis, Carolyn, and Lee-Madeline. And we were fond of the old ladies. As this story shows, I delighted in the mystery of their bonding. "Conjure Women" was first published in *Maryland Review* (1994, International Edition)

When Are They Coming?

When I became utterly serious about fiction writing circa 1991, I began to read everything I could get my hands on about writing, writers, and publishing. After reading a bit of this stuff, it dawned on me that, given my incidental place in society — a government administrator with a Ph.D. — I had garnered relationships over the years that could prove helpful to efforts to get published.

One such contact was Ms. Noma LeMoine who directed the Language Development Program for African American Students. I took three of my young adult stories to Noma and asked her if she would read them. I wanted to know how the stories might meet the needs of her program for African American literature. She read the stories, loved them, and wrote her contact at Macmillan about the stories. On the basis of that contact Macmillan's Executive Editor for Children's Books (Judith Whipple) read the three stories and loved them. In Summer 1992 she wrote me a letter asking if I would be interested in developing one or two of the stories into young adult novels. I had never attempted to write a novel, but the offer motivated me to develop one based on my story, "Me and Jer." An offshoot of the emerging novel was "When Are They Coming?"

The two young protagonists in the story are based on me and my brother Jerry, who was shot down at the age of 17 back in 1967. The other two kids, Pearl and Basil, were drummed up from a tragic event in the life of a cousin. The rest of the folks in the cafe feel very real to me. As to their origin my hunch is that I knew them early in my life, before leaving Virginia at the age of 4. In Virginia I had spent a lot of time at my Aunt Parish Monique's cafe in a town called West Point. I'm sure this place had a great impact on me. I dream of cafes and people eating, laughing, talking, and drinking bottled beer. Given the latest in brain research, I suspect the culture of that cafe may be at the center of my social, linguistic being.

Robbie the Genie

I read a lot; as most writers do. Circa 1990 I read a pinch of something about the 1839 Amistad Case in which Africans who were taken from their homeland fought to take over the ship from their captors, partly because the ship's cabin boy told them that they were going to be eaten. A couple of books on the case prompted me to write about it. Then came the Rodney King case. The idea of placing these two incidents in the same story seemed fantastical. But then in attempting to write the story, a third character, Robbie, emerged seemingly out of nowhere. And he insisted he should tell the story. While I remain unsure of Robbie's origin, I had a good time hanging out with him.

Run Low

My first ten years in South Central Los Angeles (1955-1965) were mapped out by man-made boundaries that had been created by people I did not know. The railroad tracks at Slauson Avenue were a boundary to several youth gang clusters that thrived before the Los Angeles flare-up in 1965 known as the Watts Riots. I grew up just south of Slauson Avenue near Central Avenue. On my side of the tracks were the Slausons. North of Slauson Avenue were the Businessmen (who hung out at South Park) and the Pueblos (named after a housing project). Experience taught me the potential peril of hobnobbing across the tracks — the same railroad tracks that had separated blacks and whites for years.

Sometimes we trekked across the tracks anyway. Maybe to the Bill Robinson movie theater near Vernon and Central, to Dolphins of Hollywood Record Shop. Many boys went to Upright Barbershop — Slausons and Businessmen alike had been scalped by the owner, Mr. Lewis, and both no doubt loaded up on the free penny suckers that he usually kept in a large glass jar close to his chair. The day was generally better than the night for crossing boundaries. But, according to Ray Charles, the night time was the right time to be with the one you love. Come to think of it, the main reason to cross the tracks at night was to go to a house party or to visit a girl. Both could be dangerous because of animosities that had brewed over time among rival gangs.

As a result of the Watts flare-up in Summer 1965 the old gangs ceased their rivalry. They discovered that the enemy without was worse than the one within. Everywhere I went after the riot I was called "brother." Nobody said, "Nigger, where you from?" At the age of 14 I finally got a chance to exhale.

"Run Low" is based on an incident that occurred on a day before Summer 1965. Shots were fired that day and we all ran low. The character who was shot in the story exists only in my imagination or in my subconscious in that the character, as I reflect on him now, reminds me of my brother, Jerry, whose life was snuffed out 30 years ago at the age of 17. Jerry could run fast, but sometimes he refused to. He would take a stand rather than run.

"Run Low" was awarded a $1,000 prize in *Ebony* magazine's Gertrude Johnson Williams literary contest in 1992.

Bitter Dog

While the characters are fictional composites, this story is about as close to reality as I have ever ventured in fiction. The challenge in writing this story was in recreating a manner of speaking that captured the language of my youth.

The character that comes closest to TG in real life passed away. He apparently died about three years before his family learned about it in 1997. He lived hard but, in spite of it, got in about 50 years before finally succumbing to a hard life. The shame is that he died anonymously, probably somewhere downtown Los Angeles, where I saw him, just after the 1992 Los Angeles flare-up over the Rodney King case, pushing a cart near 6th and Alvarado. I honked and he jumped, wondering seemingly if someone were out to get him. Finally he looked over at my car and recognized me. He came over and sat in the car and we talked like old times about family and friends, the way we used to while sitting on the metal rail at Slauson Park (which later became Bethune Park). At the end of our conversation he asked for a few bucks and I gave them to him along with my business card just in case he ever needed something. He called me about a month later to borrow money to hold him over until he received his government check. He never repaid me and I never expected he would.

The characters Jake and Lil Carl are based largely on a couple of old running buddies. I saw the real Jake for the first time in about 25 years at a reunion of Slauson Village. Amazing how well he looked; time had been good to him. He was married, fully employed, and lived in a nice neighborhood.

The real Lil Carl and I go way back. We attended school together, learned to appreciate jazz, and did crazy things like shave our heads clean in 8th grade only to be suspended for three days. I haven't seen him in about 25 years. But I hear about him from time to time.

Fathers and Sons

During the mid-1970s, the regulars in the neighborhood erected a makeshift shack in the parking lot of a vacated structure that had variously housed a meat market, a department store, a grocery store, and a shoe store. The shack was located near the corner of 59th Place and Hooper Avenue in Los Angeles. It was there that many of the long-standing neighborhood men — young and old, father and son, well-heeled and unemployed — played out rituals of black manhood.

This story was first published in *Obsidian II* (1994).

Gingerbread Girl

Around 1969 when I was wild, irrepressible,

18, and riding around in my first car — a 1958 Chevy Biscayne — I met a girl late one evening in the middle of a strong rain. She was a tall amazon whose smiling bulbous eyes displayed a sensual droop. After a bit of chit-chat she asked me for a ride and I drove her out to Compton, California, first to a night club and then to a bowling alley. But the ride did not stop that night. In hindsight perhaps it should have.

This is a story that cries out for answers. But it will take a novel to provide them. That novel is emerging. It's title is *The Last Dance*.